The Malaga Chronicles: The Teacher

S. L. Hemingway

Library of Congress Card Number: 2012937187

ISBN: 9781937869014

First Printing, 2012

Published by
Deer Run Press
8 Cushing Road
Cushing ME 04563

This book dedicated to Erin and her teacher and all of those from the other island who helped in its creation, in particular my wife, Nancy, who still dares to cultivate the wild flowers growing in the meadows of my heart.

TABLE OF CONTENTS

CAUTION TO THE READER

The following story is not about the struggle of those noble souls who once resided on that dot of island off the coast of Maine called Malaga. It is not a novel, history, or fantasy fiction; it is a modern dialogue in the form of folktales meant for those who believe in the *'connectedness'* of things and the unity of mankind. There was a time as children, we believed that everything we encountered from *Mom* to *chair* to the word *'more'* were all one. As our personal universe expanded we lost "touch" both literally and figuratively with truth. Human life emerged disjointed and confused, as contradiction became normal and alienation a natural condition.

It is not a coincidence that I used the story of Malaga as an example of the Diaspora of the universal human soul.

In 1912, in the same year of the Malaga tragedy, Alfred Wegener, a German, geologist, was formulating the idea that all of the continents on earth were one with his continental shift theory. It was the same year, Abdul'Baha, the son of the prophet-founder of the Baha'i Faith, was traveling across the Western World announcing the oneness of mankind.

This small book is just the first of several volumes wherein I will tell you about the *'tunnels'* that connect all of us. They are the tunnels of love, patience, trust and honor. They lay deep in the soil of our imagination. They stretch under the earth, piercing through the phantom of gases and unforgiving lava, to penetrate the ocean of the unknown that lies within all of us. I also want to acknowledge the insights of Moneveh Peters, Meridy Giles, Charles Carnegie and others in the formulation of this effort.

THE REAL MALAGA

The island of Malaga is real. You can see it while munching on a clam roll at the Sebasco Clam Shack or while lingering too long in a skiff on the water off of it, wondering why the darn waves haven't rolled you in or the swell heaved you out. In the sky the osprey hover over, wondering what wind brought them to such an ancient nest. Hearty Razorbills, pushed by easterly gales, question why they hide their eggs between the sacred rocks.

It is a small island. Narrow ledges halt at the water's edge, where once began a pasture, that reached to the mainland. The island seems to have a living bottom woven by crustaceans, mollusks and sea worms. Its beauty then comes up to the shore. Seaweed drapes the lichen-stained rocks where seagulls go to sit and Puffin whoop 'hey Al' hoping to find 'him' between the granite blocks.

The inland is virgin conifer, border-lined with birch and elm. Around them applaud an astounding audience of flowers, each one knowing when to bloom and when not. Patches of fireweed ignite where the sun hits and ants rule whatever world lies underneath.

For-the-most part the forest overflows the cup of land as if done by a generous flower arranger. Its pine needles are as soft as fern, its grass wisps of hair. It is close yet far away. From the mainland shore a boy can dream he can take a giant step and fall softly upon its leafy breast. It is so close yet away.

The Abenaki Indians emerging from the woodlands to the west saw a tall cedar growing from the sea and called the island 'Mologo'—which means cedar. The name soon became 'Malaga.' It was a place for sea hunters to drop their tangled weirs and later broken traps on its northern beach. No soul ever stayed there overnight. To the townspeople on shore it might as well have been just a big green buoy guarding boats from the rocks.

As the Nineteenth Century turned into the Twentieth, Maine took a census to find its tax base. It noticed its poor, and expelled them from its towns and villages. The family of a black man who had once owned nearby Harbor Island moved to Malaga, for who knows what reason. *Others followed: poor whites, homeless blacks, Penobscot and injured fishermen, all running away from something or running to it. Suddenly the island became human; families intersecting with families, aunts becoming sisters, newborns arriving as uncles to grown men. The island became clothed. It became a threat. As long as it remained naked, no secrets lurked within.*

Then the tragedy happened. A movement came about to cleanse Maine of it in-bred and feeble minded. In 1912, the governor took pleasure in cleaning up Malaga. He burned down homes, plowed under whatever gardens were there, dug up the graves and kidnapped the residents. Tongues around wood stoves say the real reason was that he wanted to build homes for summer people like he did on Mt. Desert Island. Good Godfrey, he tried as did others but they couldn't! No one could cleanse the island of its soul, the tales and myths, made up or not, of its now forgotten people.

Maybe I'm superstitious but not one foundation stone for 'summer people' was ever laid on the island. The following story is about that other Malaga...............

—S. L. Hemingway, 2012

THE OTHER MALAGA

CHAPTER ONE

DISMAL AND DARK THINGS

*All the powers and attributes of man are human and
hereditary in origin, outcomes of nature's processes,
except the intellect, which is supernatural.*
—Abdu'l'Baha 1912

Professor Thaddeus Mallory, one of those Darwin
people, folds himself into the rocking chair conveniently
poised on the front landing of Joe Scanlon's General
Store. Time and place? Town of Phippsburg, Midcoast
Maine, late June, a cold one at that, one the Indian calls
an Itoldyouso. His description? Well, he is beyond the
point of age guessing with graying beard and watery
eyes. You could say he has had his dose of years. His
bones sore, his lungs leaking from the short walk to the
store. To admit that he just came up in the early transit
from Brunswick hoping to catch a glimpse of the current
victims of the race improvement tea clubs, the last
inhabitants of Malaga before they were wagoned off to
the Hospital for The Feeble Minded in New Gloucester
would not be a lie, but to confess as to why he really
made the trip would be a betrayal to that thing he held
the closest and dearest to him, his sanity.

In his fist shakes a mug of Farmers coffee, brewed in
a pot that hadn't seen a wash in weeks, just the way it
tasted when he was a young boy down in Millinocket. It
is a fair compensation for arriving late and missing the
pageantry of feigned farewells from the Phippsburg town
folks.

No one would know it was deliberate. Joe, the father

1

of one of his former students at Bowdoin, who operates the town's general store, fills him up to the brim with the account, like he had filled his cup of coffee, with a satisfied grin.

Unlike the previous weeks when the first group of residents of the island were rounded up amid the fanfare of reporters from the Portland Times, the Boston Press, the Maine Governor's entourage and various self appointed women's eugenics committees, the atmosphere had been less official. That day, the last group to be pulled out were children clinging to half-dressed mothers, and old men barely on the arms of old women. To witness the tragedy now, there were only flanks of jeering boys and amused town people some applauding good riddance, others tossing pails of water to symbolize cleansing. Nearing the end of the event someone spotted a lanky black man in the backwater on a raft laden with makeshift furniture attempting to reach the mouth of the river. The crowd broke out in laughter. Upon hearing it, the black man's stroke quickened and he lost his balance. The raft, furniture and all, tipped over. Just a few in the crowd hunched forward as if to help him from that far distance. Others just closed their eyes as the dark man struggled to recapture a box and an armchair before they floated up the river towards West Bath without him.

"Yup, finally got rid of the blight, Professor. Town was the shame of Maine with that island stuck next to us the way it is. Yup, shame!"

"Shame of Maine?" Mallory repeats but with a different tone, placing his mug between his knees leaving a hand free to stroke his beard.

As he does his eyeglasses drop lower on his thin nose

so he raises his middle finger to both push it back and to make a point. "Joe don't you think that when the raft tipped over and no one helped the poor colored, as you tell it—that was not the real shame of Maine?' "

"Yup, you missed a good cleansing there. Hoped more Portland folks would be down here for the event, stocked up for it too! "

Joe's large head turns toward the island. It looks like a multicolored rock. Spring had always left it with a gown of colors.

"Got a bet with my dog Cleveland going that they make that there place into a summer rest spot like they're doing up in Freeport!"

Mallory just smiles thinly. He is a Professor of History at ivy-covered Bowdoin and a doctorate from Harvard. He had known whole civilizations ignore the color of their demise even though it was right there in crimson red beneath them.

What does one man, or a tiny town hanging from the coast of Maine, know from a bean supper for that matter? Mallory reaches in his penny pocket and comes up with ten cents and offers it quickly to Joe.

"Gosh, don't have to do that Professor, not after all what you done for my Tommy!"

Joe pushes Mallory's smooth hand away. He notices the hand trembles ever so slightly. Joe is an expert at hands after all; it is the hand that holds the money, not the patron's smile, words, or promises. Sometimes a patron would say one thing and the hand would say another.

"Sides I like talking to an educated man, at least once this side of winter. I like to think if my Tommy had come back from Cuba he'd be ending up like you, a professor or something like that. Me not understanding a word he said but still loving him. 'Sides I consider the likes of you my friend."

The professor recalls again that golden haired Tommy was one of those golden haired heroes that T.R. himself didn't bring back from Havana—he was one of the ones who transferred to Manila and left for the bugs of Luzon. That was over a decade ago. As he asks himself if it had been that long, his lips move a little. Joe considers it a positive response.

Had he known Joe all those years? It surprised him. Most of his "modern" friends (as he called those he met on this side of the 20th Century) hadn't lasted that long. He had befriended some of the greatest minds north of Cambridge and somehow they reduced themselves to acquaintances and now here was a man, ignorant by his own account, opinionated beyond words, and bigoted to his core who considers himself a friend.

And all they had in common were a name on a term paper and pots of coffee, shared infrequently when he was in the area. Besides in his estimation Joe's son was a fruit that didn't fall far from the tree.

Tommy barely made it to his sophomore year. He had failed his section on Pliny when patriotism conveniently got hold of him just after the mid-year exams. In a way, Mallory held himself partly responsible for Tommy's death. At times he thought that just with a little more compassion and patience Tommy could have turned it around.

Joe pauses expecting a reciprocal declaration of friendship but that moment awkwardly passes when a thin, red headed, rather good-looking woman wrapped in a wispy grey mantilla boards the store's porch. The professor, startled at her sudden appearance, draws back in embarrassment. His empty coffee mug falls from his lap as he attempts to stand. Upon recognizing her, Joe puts on his shopkeeper's finest smile then he hesitates not knowing what her response would be.

"Good 'ay, Miss 'em!"

He didn't expect her to be out and about that day, especially that day. He thought with the Malaga cause lost, she would be shut up in her big house for a month or down in Massachusetts trying to find another cause with which to rile up decent folks.

"Well, Mister Scanlon, you won, dare not say anything more!" The woman angrily turns away from the shopkeeper, and finds herself facing the Professor's rump as he is bending down to pick up the mug. "Oh, excuse me!"

"Mrs. Shapleigh, only good sense won here," announces Joe.

"Good sense, barbaric, more like barbaric sense!" She whips back.

Feeling like a referee who stumbles upon a duel between unknown circumstances and purpose, the professor reaches out his hand toward the woman as he rises and announces: "Scanlon looks like I have to introduce myself, before what appears to be a boxing match begins. Madame my name is Thaddeus Mallory."

"Good sense, barbaric, more like barbaric sense!" she repeats.

"Professor Thaddeus Mallory, from Bowdoin, the professor might add but he's wicked shy about things like that," emphasizes Joe wishing he could pick up Mallory by the collar to use him as a shield against his opponent's verbal agility.

"Ordinarily, I would wait to be introduced to a male who seems to be a gentleman. To avoid having to be introduced by this barbarian, not by a long shot will I wait. Name is Shirley Shapleigh, Miss Shapleigh, never been married. I say that with an element of pride." Shirley pulls her shawl back revealing a handsome woman, not at all elderly, but aged in the glow of youth in such a way that powder and creams would only mask. If beauty could trail along with years she would be the benefit of it. Anger could never fit her face although her eyes—as blue as they could be—are overcast with it. The redness is still there from many evenings of tears.

"I didn't come here for you to gloat Scanlon, I came here for a tin of tea...you know Ceylon mixed with a little bit of the black mountain leaf kind."

As Scanlon and his customer examine the tins of obvious oriental design, Mallory watches her. He couldn't imagine that a woman with so much bearing could be an inhabitant of Phippsburg let alone this far north in Maine. During his years in Cambridge he had witnessed women transform into "ladies."

Yet, Miss Shapleigh could not be defined so easily, "ladies" had acquired a softness of purpose in every movement and conversation.

In the description "ladies," rested a desire for conformity, to mold into whatever a man wanted even though it could never be achieved.

Miss Shapleigh moved deliberately, shoulders back, not like most women who at all times desired to be erased from the moment.

Even with 100 percent of her attention on her tea purchase Shirley could feel Mallory's eyes with her back.

Dismal and Dark Things

It is a surprise to both men, perhaps even herself, when she suddenly swirls around and asks: "So, a Bowdoin man?" The tea spoon tips into the professor's coffee mug.

Miss Shapleigh wants to laugh but the professor's face is so solemn she isn't sure if he even noticed.

"Actually, I did my degrees at Harvard."

"He teaches at Bowdoin, Miss Shapleigh. My son was studying there. That other place Har—vard up in My-Ass-U-Shit is the school where the folk have no taste for good coffee. They even put cream in their tea. I know plenty of them that come from My-Ass-U-Shit!" Joe inserts quickly just as the professor takes a sip from his mug.

"Mister Scanlon...there is a lady present!" The professor scolds while biting his tongue to avoid announcing his own version of a gentleman's obscenity.

"Speaking of taste," with a tinge of amusement Shirley interjects. "What are you doing in this God-forsaken place? Wait a minute! You came here for the Spectacle."

"Spectacle?"

"Yes, spectacle, 'semel in anno licet insanire,' there is a little madness and shame in all of us that has to be let out once in a while. Poppa used to say that," she paused, "too many times."

"Spectacle?"

"You came because everyone else at the Faculty Club has already visited this God-forsaken town to witnesses the eviction of human beings from their homes, from some would say, their world. You've come so you too can go back and talk about it over your coffee and sweet rolls then go onto international politics and the tragedy of

Germany's Bismarck and his appetite for devouring innocent little kingdoms before your own dinner is served!"

"Gosh, Professor, I should've warned you," Joe whispers. "Miss Shapleigh was the teacher at that island's school and she's a string short in the corset too."

"You're not from here, then?" Mallory asks, ignoring Joe completely.

"No, Southern Maine, in a more civilized place. In my opinion it is the part that in some way or another never broke away from Massachusetts."

"You must be devastated. You must have known the families intimately?" questions Mallory.

"I knew their hearts." She then gives the professor her long silence. The kind of silence the wind gives the trees as it combs the forest shaking loose dead leaves and branches from their hiding places so that all can see.

"Dear Professor Mallory," Miss Shirley Shapleigh takes her breath and continues, "that Faculty Club of yours if I am not mistaken lies just 100 yards from the house of Harriet Beecher Stowe. You do know about the intrepid woman who wrote *Uncle Tom's Cabin*, I hope? Or are you one of those scientists who measure the shapes of heads to determine if they are of the superior type? You should be devastated too! Anyhow you can always tell a Bowdoin man but you can't tell him much!"

"Miss Shapleigh, I think you're being a little bit out of sorts, that I don't blame you for being, you know, owing to the circumstances." Mallory replies awkwardly.

Joe slaps the board with her tab attached on the counter. She quickly signs it, picks up the tea tin and rushes away.

Dismal and Dark Things

"Uncle Tom's Cabin?" Before the look of bewilderment leaves Joe's face, Professor Thaddeus Mallory disappears too. Joe is alone. He rubs the back of his right ear lobe, a habit he acquired from his father to announce to the world he was thinking.

"Uncle Tom's Cabin?" Joe repeats it as he slides the glass display case containing the special tea into its home on the wall. It hit him like a blizzard of no see 'ems in June.

He remembers when he was just a fresh boy down in that school in Bath they made him read a book about a nigger who had a cabin deep in the dismal woods of the South.

All the girls in class were bringing tears to the situation when Miss Soule, *a cutie she was,* Joe thought, read it out loud to the whole class. The Great War was fought over it. Joe lost two uncles, the ones he liked, in that darn war and who knows how many distant on his mother's side. Uncle Tom and that damn cabin of his held dismal and dark things.

Quickly Joe moves to the doorway of his store. He can make out a slither of Malaga's coast hugging its rocks and lobsters traps in the distance.

He can just make out an angled roof that is more oak than slate. He stares hard and long. Maybe dismal things still grow in those cabins? Regardless tomorrow is July 1st and George is going to go over there in the morning and burn down what's left of things.

***

Mallory at first tries to catch up to Miss Shapleigh, but she is in a determined track lunging forward, ignoring the unusually cordial acquaintances she passes on the road.

Just as Mallory is about to call out to her, no doubt with an apology of sorts, a tiny mulatto boy runs up to her and slips a weathered cloth covered book into her bosom.

It seems to be as much a surprise to him as it is to her, because as soon as he makes his delivery he looks up and slams into Mallory. The professor loses his balance and lands on the recently dried mud road. A small crowd of town folk surrounds him. An overgrown teen in a red plaid shirt grabs the small boy.

"Let him go, it was more like I ran into him than the visa-versa!"

Mallory feels a lace sleeve on the side of his cheek. It remains there until others hands lift him upright.

"Let him go!" the professor demands.

"Yes! He was just returning something that belongs to me," Miss Shapleigh quickly announces. The bully releases the tiny boy who disappears behind the row of houses from which he somehow appeared.

"See stranger here is no worse for wear that he didn't take your wallet or much more. See got reason to get rid of them!"

A woman's voice rises with the others swirling around him.

"Hope you got a wicked dose of shame for your friend here Miss Shapleigh, for what you were not teaching them in that school of yours," another voice joins the others.

"We will get them all, Mister. Some are squatting like birds in West Bath in a field down there."

"Don't mind them Miss Shapleigh, I am all right. Yet I cannot see how you could be all right, having to have to endure all of this backwardness."

Dismal and Dark Things

At that Miss Shirley Shapleigh just smiles and pats the back of his hand. She leads the slightly disheveled educator to a black dented Jackson Model C, lately bequeathed from her father, which is hugging a railing on the other side of the road.

"So far so good, as are the plans of mice and fishermen." She whispers to herself as she jumps on to the vehicle's brass trimmed running board.

CHAPTER TWO

STRANGE HOSPITALITY

The Shapleigh manse sits on a knoll overlooking Cundy's Harbor which is just one of a hundred harbors which groove the face of the Midcoast of Maine. Like the house, the Shapleigh's were a secretly inherited clan slipping across history with deeds and mortgages all the way down to the New Hampshire border. Mallory notices the chaotic arrangement of spring flowers and early weeds surrounding the path. Shrub honey-suckle and sweet purple lupine flow up to the massive stone steps above which presides the black oak front door. His mother was into flowers and things of that sort and would have disapproved of such a display of poorly pruned nature as an adequate welcoming sign.

After Shirley deposits the professor in the sitting room she slips into one of the adjoining spaces while in mid-sentence her voice moves in several octaves.

"When does your transportation...my hasn't it gotten cold...I hope you like exotic tea...my brother is one of your Ivy Clan....New Haven... he wanted to get as far away from this place as possible....it's amazing that Scanlon even carries the dull assortment that he does carry."

Mallory just exhales a barely audible "Yes," his eyes capturing his surrounding like they do when they wander in a Boston museum. Both ceiling and woodwork are of dark bog oak as if in one continuous motion an ancient tree was scooped out of its pulp and laid on top of oriental rugs.

A mixture of Victorian and French chairs and small

cushions led to a fireplace trimmed with red mahogany and gold leaf. A red velvet divan reigns in a corner. Several paintings adorn the wall. Heavy green drapes shelter the contents of the room from the harshness of the day.

His eyes fall on a water lily cherry wood side table where the weathered cloth book which Shirley received from the Mulatto boy sits next to an impressive brass carriage clock.

"Well, Professor, when did you say your transit was scheduled to take you back to Brunswick?" Shirley reenters the room holding a tray upon which sits a rosette porcelain tea pot and two ugly clay mugs. "I know what you're thinking—the mugs. They don't fit the arrangement of all of this....room and all. You see that's why I like them because they don't fit. Very Maine, you know."

"By 2 P.M. they should be rounding up the horses. I would have much preferred coming down on motor car but the Bath Road is still ditched out from last week's rain storm."

"Two? Almost two now, you'll miss it. You shouldn't be in town at night these days." She pours the tea and hands the mug to him.

"Why did you agree to come home with me? Am I that intriguing?"

"You invited me, Miss Shapleigh, and you do hold some part of the mystery I came here to understand."

"Mystery! You are a stranger, that's the reason why I invited you....a stranger whose morality is not known or motives challenged by those little people in their little minds.

"My how the tongues out there must be wagging, my grand mere use to say, 'Like winter feed mares in a bach-

elor's cow barn.' A teacher in an automobile with someone male other than her father and taking him home at
that! This town sees me as the Spinster of Bats anyhow...some of those who have been in the house say that
I hang upside down from that chandelier up there on
occasion."

Both are drawn to the center of the ceiling. A glass
menagerie of shapes suspend above. Shirley laughs. The
professor sees just a lighting fixture. Shirley sees it as
the sun of her private world of books and journals. If
clouds could roam freely up and down the ceiling she
wouldn't be surprised, even if a finch flew past.

"Is it haunted?" It is a question he didn't want to
admit to himself but it fell from his lips.

"Silly, it hasn't been electrified yet...still comes down
for lighting like in the olden days."

"No, I mean the island. Is it haunted?"

Upon hearing that question Shirley sits. Amazement
spreads across her face that quickly turns into a wide
smile.

"Sir, you came here not to see those unfortunate
souls tossed out of their homes like boxes, but to see if
their stories are true?"

Mallory hesitates. The truth is that he had visited
Phippsburg many times before to observe in an extreme-
ly unscientific way the habits of the strange folk who
called Malaga their home.

He never went to their island itself, and barely spoke
to one of the inhabitants, except in the everyday
sequencing of necessities, such as unloading his lug-
gage, removing his dinner plate, yielding to him as he
entered the roadway. He thought his information could
be obtained from those who had a more intimate, daily

relationship with them.

The truth is that he had always been fascinated with certain stories that circulated down as far as Brunswick. One of their clan, Henry Johnson fought in the Civil War yet he appeared only approaching fifty years old when he served the professor a bowl of clam chowder in the faculty dining room fifty years after the war. Another was Mallory's recent scholarship on the late General O. Howard. In an attempt to write the illustrious man's sketch for the reader's page in the *Boston Sunday Advertiser* for much needed income he had stumbled upon a connection with the island that Howard claimed turned around his ill-fated career. Even the Scanlon boy arrived at school as a consummate bully but by his second year barely spoke before he became patriotic. He told his classmates that he had been cursed by the Negroes on Malaga. He shared with some of his friends that he heard Scott Joplin's "Maple Leaf Rag" playing over and over again in his sleep, not that he would have preferred "Chopsticks." Now in spite of Howard's and the Scanlon boy's experiences what concerns him most is that unspeakable newspaper article he wrote so long ago that he thought was the cause of the current misery.

"Their stories are their souls, Professor Mallory. I taught their children for five years and the only thing I know about them is that! When you think of it, so isn't it for us all. The Romans were their history, the British their biographies and us Americans, like it or not, we are our fiction." Shirley continues to sip her Ceylon. Her eyebrows arch, cheeks bemused as she watches Mallory, like a bird of prey but instead of for meat, for emotion.

"Real shame is not that these poor people are forced to leave their world behind, it's that people like us do not even think of them as human," Shirley continues. "To the average one of us they are ogres, gremlins, which cast spells and eat their children, and I dear say, eat each other!"

The professor quickly looks down as if the real purpose of his trip to Phippsburg had not been already revealed and shame associated with it. He did not think about the fact that the superstition about the island had grown out of fear and racial prejudice.

Shirley places a palm on Mallory's shoulder. He can feel the lace from her sleeve touching his neck. Such a motion immobilizes him. It is like an injection of sympathy, a hormone unfamiliar to him at that age.

"I have seen you before you know, sitting on Mrs. Anderson's boarding house porch looking over at the island...for several years." Shirley admits. "I thought you were someone from say *Harper's,* or one of those new sociologists looking for ways to save them."

She rises and walks through the sunlight breaking around the thick drapes. Upon reaching the cherry wood side table she picks up the cloth book and returns. "So what did you find out, Professor Malloy?"

"I never got up enough nerve to get to know what they were all about. I'd sit there for a couple days, wonder, and then head back to Massachusetts where I tutored stubborn brats Latin for the summer," the professor confesses.

"Don't look so much a pity. I am not saying that every story I have heard from those poor folk who lived on Malaga had an explanation.

After all, I found that they lived in another world with its own laws of gravity and sense of time. It was a world that was there even before they existed."

Shirley, sitting on a French chair that belonged more in a garden patio than in its present surroundings, looks up at the professor and opens the book.

"Frankly, Professor, I didn't believe in anything at all, even God, before I took the position of mistress of their poor pathetic schoolhouse."

"What happened, Miss Shapleigh?"

"This book happened."

***

Mallory reaches out for the slim volume. He scans the pages, seeing nothing of interest and hands it back to her.

"Four years ago in the spring I found it on that table in the cabin they called a schoolhouse. When I came in late one morning having to have to row myself in because the man the County Board hired to do it was too drunk to even find the oars. It had only one story in it then, one very primitive story." Shirley's whole body seems to be intent to be spread into the past and after a few moments of silent breathing that's where she goes. A thin page leaps to her fingertips and she reads:

One ancestor, in the time the island was lost after it was found to be lost, was called the Teacher because he found it again. He knew everything because he came from the tunnel. So when the island got lost he used his mystical powers to find it. Now all the children and all of the ma's and the pa's were joyful and afraid at the same time because being lost they knew, but being found they always wanted.

But he was an old man even then. They reasoned if he died who would find the island if it got lost again? They told the Ancestor of their fears. He pondered a bit and said: "I will grow a tree in the middle of the island and tether it to Paradise so when I go the island will stay put. You will call this tree Teacher and if another one comes along chest puffing up carrying two paper bags which in one is what he calls a lunch and in the other, the one that is weeping something sticky, he calls knowledge, be wary, especially if this new teacher's feet do not have any roots!"

Well, it came a time when Old Man died and the tree called Teacher didn't grow anymore and the children got tired of climbing it and the ma's and the pa's grew tired of brushing its leaves from the roofs. One day a new teacher did come. He wore eyeglasses, had a vest on, and was fitted with a wig and just like the old man prophesied; he carried two paper bags. One had his lunch and the other one, a mystery.

At first everyone, even the dogs, were wary of him but time went on and because he said that he was going to teach the people of the island new things, a lot of them warmed up to him. Eventually, even the top of the tree withered and what tethered it to the Almighty fell down like a baby letting go its cord. And true to his word the new teacher taught the children things they could not feel or want to feel and for the ma and pa's, things they could not see or ever see. There came a time when nobody wanted to look out at the sea anymore, all they wanted to do was to look at the land yonder, wanting to grow things and own the things they learned about. It was so bad that no one, even the teacher, looked out over from Mary's perch. Now if someone had they would have seen the dark clouds crawling down from the North or heard the warnings of the old man's ghost in the thunder.

Strange Hospitality

Then the storm came and spat out its anger churning day into night and East into West. Soon the island became lost again. Those who were left on the island didn't know what to do.

First they called the Ancestor, but he didn't come and then they looked for the tree, but the tree was down from the storm lying on its side with roots still intact. Finally they call the new teacher but he didn't come. Even when things calmed down they looked for the teacher, but still they couldn't find him. They looked everywhere, even reported him so he wouldn't get any pay. You see it was just like the old man said, "When it comes to teaching, if your feet don't have any roots, one day you'll be washed away."

***

The professor's face reddens. The story hit a nerve. He knew his own roots were questionable and only the Lord knew what was in his own paper bag. "How dare those superstitious fools try to teach a teacher how to teach?" he blustered.

"Not at all, to the contrary, I found it very instructive. As much as I could, I shared my lessons with the children at the base of the tall cedar in the middle of the island. In the winter months we lit the classroom fires with some of its twigs, until I found a way to attach ink pen nips to them which enabled them to write with perfect penmanship! By the way," she continued as if reading his thoughts, "I'd rather have roots than a mystery in a paper bag."

Feeling for some reason less threatened by the implication of the story, the professor is embarrassed that such a novice teacher had such a positive and effective reaction.

"That was quite innovative, if I must say so myself. How did you ever become a teacher, and here above all places?"

"Where else can a woman go and do these days even in the new Twentieth Century. Cleaning cobwebs out of children's minds or as a nurse cleaning whatever they call it between old men's toes?"

Mallory clears his throat, uncomfortably shifting his feet.

"Sir, I didn't start off as desiring to be a teacher, I wanted to be in politics." Without even waiting for the professor's reaction she stands walks over to the tea pot and refreshes her mug and offers it to her guest with Maine etiquette: "Warmer upper?"

"What about the other paper bag?"

"Other bag?" Shirley paused.

"The other paper bag the teacher carried, the one with the mystery?"

"Oh, that. The children told me that they found the teacher a couple years later digging clams on Bailey's Island. He was putting the mystery to good use. You see, God's bad penmanship got the teacher bringing boots, not roots, to the island. When it comes to following the lesson plan, once a teacher, always a teacher!

"Warmer upper? I'm not asking for the vote or anything. All I want to do is help make a change in the world."

The professor wants to respond but having had his own clashes with aggressive Suffragettes in the past didn't know where this conversation was leading.

"Don't worry Professor I am not trying to nudge you into a discussion where you or no man could ever win. I wasn't talking about that voting thing. I wanted to do something to end war, to ban starvation, resolve the inequities in mankind, you know what I mean!"

"Are you one of those sentimental women? If you are, you sure fooled me!"

"No, just the contrary to sentimental, I am practical, very much so. That's how it all started with me being here at all. The girls and I were in Boston attending a talk given by the American Anti-Imperialist League. The speaker was Josephine Shaw Lowell. During the questioning period I asked her how I could be like her, especially in her efforts to halt the cruel expansion of our country into the Philippines, and stop the massacres of the poor and the innocent. She told me I should first try to stop the massacres of the poor and innocent where I live. I was surprised. I wasn't aware of any 'poor and innocent' where I was from. That's when she told me to find them and teach them. I did. I found Malaga. Even then I didn't understand what was happening here would affect events that were happening thousands of miles away. A couple of months after I began my mission here I realized that the secret of the connectedness of things is justice. I came in one morning, the book was open and this story was in it."

CHAPTER THREE

JUSTICE

FENCES

At first they thought
They were angels
That their feathers
Were wings
But only when they sold
The angels
They found out
They couldn't
Sing..........

Now in those days it was not strange to see an Indian looking like a dried up corn husk watching the wasting away of the universe, this to him would have been the lands south of the Kennebec.

The Mic Mac, the Penobscot, the Abenaki, the Passamaquoti, all the original people, some with osprey feathers matted on woven shoots in their hair, others with pointed hoods made of bark wood, most times cedar skin that looked like shrouds, they all had leathered eyes wrinkled to the pupil. They had seen so much that they did not say much and when they did, the wind in the oak and pine grew silent. That is why when eighty-year-old Sokois, wisest sachem of the Dog People, said, "Dead!" in 'naki talk, the sun seemed to come from under its cloud to listen.

"Dead?" the old leathered Indian spat, as Obadiah Landers repeatedly stabbed his spade into the earth.

Justice

"Dead?"

Obediah was a fat, red-faced English farmer who was staking out part of the land the Plymouth Company had granted him the previous year. The land cupped Casco Bay near the New Meadows River sixty miles northeast of the garrison which was later to become the town of Portland.

With every thrust, the old Indian's body trembled thinking that it was witnessing the stabbing of a loved one so that the fowl body of one of the strange white men could poison what was left of the marked spot.

The previous year, Sokois had grown his corn on this section of the tract. This year an Englishman on a horse warned him that soon he would have to move closer to the Indian settlement in the west on the Penobscot. Then the Mic Mac boy with the man told him that even his shadow upon that land which he now cast, where his father and his father's father had cast for centuries, would not exist anymore. Old Sokois could not believe it. He just shook his head and laughed.

"Where Dead?" the old Indian repeated, this time pointing to the grassy hill where the Englishman's farmhouse stood. Landers, his forehead beading sweat, ignored him as he continued to hammer stakes into ground.

In the past, he would have never ignored Sokois. His family depended upon the Indian for their survival.

Sokois opened to him some of the secrets of the new world. The old Naki had taught him how to fish, hunt for fowl and venison, and how to cure his children with berries and roots. Once Landers had the questions, lots of questions but now it was the Indian's turn to ask the questions. To the Original People in those days important questions were only asked of the Great Spirit and an answer was not expected.

Furthermore, to the Dog People to speak even one word in English was painful. Its meaning was always used to their disadvantage. In the white man's tongue meaning was one thing one moment and the exact opposite the next.

The white man was silent now but Sokois knew white men were never silent. There was a restless tongue always speaking in their brains. That is why when Obadiah spoke the Indian never listened to the words from his mouth; the old man only heard the words that hid in white man's eyes.

"Little one... gone?" Sokois cradled his arms with sympathy.

Startled by the question and after a long pause, Obadiah finally understood what the old man was getting at.

"No Sokois, Baby John is in bonny good health. The whole family is, God bless us!"

"Then why you kill the earth with sticks that grow nothing, and make nothing?"

"Making something, God bless us!" Landers stopped from what he was doing, he did not look up when he realized that he was using the Lord's name in vain.

"Doing a fence, Good Jesus! We're doing a fence!"

The Indian knew only four legged creatures needed fences. For the two legged, the Great Sachem made water and mountains to contain them.

Yet he heard of land in the South among the Massachusetts where white people placed sticks around land, upon which Indians could not walk, plant seed or even stand.

Justice

"Land dead, me here no more?" Suddenly, the old Mic Mac saw the vision of a golden bird pulling a fish across the mountains just where the day's sun goes down and never gets up like what must happen at the end of time.

Obadiah looked up, wiping his forehead. His moist face was stern, his thin lips tight, and his eyes shouting their truth to the old man.

"Not just you, friend, no one can, Indian nor white without my favor. This is my land now!" He stood up, steadied himself and with a swing of his mallet buried a post deep into one of the many holes he had dug.

"I sit by these waters long time watching. My father sits there, my son sits there. See them!"

Obadiah's torso twisted in the direction of the Indian. The Indian's arm stretched out like a wand across Obadiah's eyes revealing the small land mass in the bay. On it he could make out emerald tinted cedars rising above drying trees and bushes in the weak light of that late fall afternoon.

"Friend, you still think your father and your son may be buried there?" Obadiah said although his eyes said he knew the Indian's son Wannasobec, while helping him in the fields months before, was killed by two men who while passing the fields mistook the boy for a thief. In a panic, Obadiah had helped them for fear that the desperate men might have turned on him and his family.

The farmer could not bear to tell the old Indian that his son had been murdered by men like himself struggling to keep square the lives of their own brood in what to them was a cruel, transplanted homeland. So he suggested to Sokois that traders kidnapped his son and sold him to a plantation in the Barbados where there was sun and healing salt air.

"This sacred place, you say come here no more?" Sokois lamented.

It was then Obadiah remembered that the Abenaki always came to that spot to stare at the island, which they called Mologo. It was the place of the cedar tree, where spirits of the restless become bark skin and the tree's trunk becomes a canoe to the afterlife. He heard that all tortured souls journeyed to it and became part of the tree.

"You can have leave to rest here friend, but your wait must be over yonder, where the boulder lies, beyond the fence. But don't do your watching on Captain Robert's land,"

Obadiah advised. He knew the captain hated Indians and was planning to erect fencing vowing to oversee every yard of it with muskets.

Quickly he went back to his chore. He dragged timber from their pile and raising them slid them into their resting places. He did this as the Indian watched and waited.

Soon the Indian's eyes became weights on his back. He stopped working, turned to meet the deep-furrowed face of Sokois.

"Trust me, I be doing it for your own good. It will be like me home in Yorkshire. A pretty sight: rolling hills, down to meadows so thick you could swim in them, gillyflowers, red and pink sneaking from the trellises and peas with buds stringing above the lettuce row.

Everything, even this dirt will have the smell of home; that is the home before the landlords stole the common land from beneath us like pushing a whole nation of us off a sheer cliff, and we came to this unknown country hoping Jesus' grace would come with us."

There was no comment just a long silence between breaths. Obadiah then thought about the time when he first arrived in the colony. He witnessed the hanging of an Indian for stealing.

The drummer who had accused him was using the opportunity to sell his wares to the attending crowd. 'Tis the New England Way,' the drummer whispered to him with a broad smile. Obadiah soon learned it meant that one should take advantage of every opportunity one can. 'A good hanging brings folks together and opens their pocket books!' the drummer whispered.

The New England Way was how he had lived his life ever since. He built a corn mill outside the Praying Indians' village of Natick and unfairly profited from the new converts to Christianity.

He brewed mash and sold it in the village. He transported gun powder in corn flour sacks to outlaw tribes on the Mohawk. Finally, when a kiln of hot brew tipped over on the inebriated child (barely six years if a day) tending it, the church people forced him and his family out of the settlement. After that, he applied and negotiated a grant of land in the Northern outposts.

"Understand this, my friend, the utmost feeling me have for you savages." Obadiah broke the silence as he returned to the rudely dug furrow where piles of dirt dotted along posts waiting for their rails. The old Indian looked down on him without emotion as Obadiah rambled to himself.

"Why when I was in Natick I did well by you people. Employed them, did I, even the young 'uns. They brought me grain. I, for one, didn't care from whence it came. I would do it in and give it back to them at a fair price.

"They took up Jesus Christ you know, but most thought Jesus was the so-called pious John Eliot, a pale man like me with his own sweet swindle. He told his so-called flock that they had souls, heathen with souls!

"He earned a pretty bob and pee from the Long Parliament for that. That's how the trouble and strife began. 'Can't be a slave and a brother at the same time,' says Genesis. And after that not a one of them wanted to work, just pray."

At that, Obadiah paused and with guilt he looked up. "You think you have a soul?"

Not expecting an answer the white man returned to his work. "Of course, you don't. If you did, you would know what I mean and you would have one. None of you have souls. Your son, where ever he is, does not have a soul!"

Obadiah stood, his hand motioning to a split log which crossed behind the old man. "Help me with that!" he commanded, reaching toward Sokois. Whether the Indian thought the white man was attacking him or whether he thought that Obadiah had asked him to become a part of the murder of his way of life by helping, no one knows.

He struck the white man. Stunned and unable to regain his balance Obadiah fell backwards landing on the ground. Fumbling, the white man's hand reached for the spade which he thought was somewhere beside him. Instead, the hand fell into one of the mounds of displaced earth. It pulled out a small tarnished silver bowl. Obadiah clutched it. Surprised he sat up his thumbs quickly rubbing away the dirt encrusted in its engravings, a bird's wing wrapped around its circumference.

Between its outlined feathers stretched inlaid jewels, in the inner lip glimpses of gold glinted through the green discolored haze of decay. Stuck to the base of the bowl were black and white shell beads fashioned to the form of a necklace. The white farmer forgot about the struggle for his own life moments before and excitedly began digging.

Suddenly, he remembered the struggle. He straightened up to refocus when he did he noticed that the old Indian was holding the beads clinging to the cup with dried blood, as tears filled the old man's eyes.

"Heathen, what do you know about this?" Stumbling forward, Obadiah snatched the cup and beads from the old Indian's gnarled hands.

"White man, what do you know about this?" Sokois eyes said. He knew the beads were his son's and he also knew of the white man's thirst for treasure regardless of what it was.

Sokois' tears dried to laughter. He now knew what the digging was all about. He reached out and pulled the beads off the cup. And as great wise men do he prayed and then he flung his arms wide open, pointing to Malaga Island and announced: "Great, Much!"

"Take me there, heathen!" The farmer shouted with words dripping in greed.

For years it had been rumored that pirates having Dutch authority had plundered Spanish galleons during the European War and buried their treasure on the coast of the North Atlantic land mass. It was not unusual to see Spanish visitors with their ruffled sleeves and flat lace collars in the area seeking to reclaim what was stolen. This was particularly true after a Spanish coin or two were taken in by a Portsmouth tradesman.

It was not known then, even hundreds of years later that in an attempt to mislead others as to the location of their loot, the privateers, who in on the truth and enamored with puzzles, designated their treasure to the spot called Malaga; Malaga off the coast of rocks of Maine, not the one on the sun fortress of the Mediterranean in Spain.

As both men approached the island in a birch bark canoe, one's heart was drained of hope while the other's was filled with apprehension. Obadiah knew that if he found treasure there, his life and that of his family's would never be the same.

The world would come, the strangers and the Spanish and the lawyers and the riff-raff with their New England Way and the fences wouldn't mean much anymore. But it would be a secret, he said to himself over and over again, his secret. Yet he, even himself, could not be trusted. On one cold winter with his home blanketed with sickness and hunger, he would trade the silver bowl and eventually, the truth of whatever he found on the island for any comfort he could afford for his family. He knew if there was treasure he could never return. Sokis knew it too, there was justice in it.

The canoe slid up on the beach and the two men stood—Obadiah holding the silver bowl, Sokios clutching his son's shell necklace. Then they alighted. The surrounding trees darkened when they did, the wind shut its flowers tight, the boulders rolled over the cranny spaces, and bittersweet opened a path for them through the strangled pine.

Reports surfaced that reached all the way to Boston not long after Obadiah Landers' disappearance; farmers saw Indians tearing down fences and urinating in unplowed ridges in the Casco area.

For ten years the land remained open. Fearing an uprising, Captain Roberts moved his family to the garrison at Sturgeon Creek. For ten years an Indian could see miles down the pastures alongside the bay without seeing any fences.

Moreover, if he stood on the spot where Sokois use to stand and looked out at the island of Mologo, now called Malaga, he might have been able to make out the giant cedar with the face of a white man dancing with ancestor's spirit on the surface of its bark and if he listened carefully through the living waves, he could hear the music of justice.

***

Shirley Shapleigh closes the book, her eye lids follow. The professor opens his eyes, sees her in a moment of contemplation then exhales when he is sure she is breathing.

"Did they find treasure?"

Shirley, mustering a broad smile, shrugs.

"That's a tale of some interest, but I dare say only to a romantic." Mallory stands and assumes a college lecturer posture. "It's far from scientific in an historical sense. There was no treasure on that piece of land am I not right? Treasure and privateers rarely roamed these waters. " Mallory carefully sips his tea thinking of ways to shift the topic but failing miserably. "My dear lady, what is the point of the story?"

"Professor, folk tales are not supposed to always make sense? Among other things they are meant to expand our world of possibility.

"In the story both men face the reality of change. The Mic Mac's fear is from exactly the same reason why

Obadiah left England which was exclusion from God's common land.

"Now the old Indian's fear is more immediate. But Obadiah, who knows what the loss of freedom means, fears that when the boundaries are not post and rail, they become greed, corruption, the loss of privacy, and ultimately the loss of honor. "

"What happened to the two men?"

"Simple, they became one. Suffering in Manila Bay is suffering in Cundy's Harbor. Like that colored spiritual All God's Children Got a Robe!...a robe of suffering that is. If it is the treasure you came for Professor, you will be disappointed!" She returns the book to its station on the table then looks up with that all-knowing smile all women know but will not admit to.

"Treasure hardly, my dear lady," he replied while thinking, Who is this woman beside me? Why is she there offering kindness? Does she know it was my actions that caused all of this misery to the people she undoubtedly loves? I thought it would be so straightforward. Now, Shirley Shapleigh has come into my life.

CHAPTER FOUR

COMPASSION

It is the mention of Obadiah's silver bowl that reminds Shirley of refreshments. What woman of her times did not make that an excuse to rearrange herself out of the gaze of a member of the opposite sex? Upon returning with an assortment of cheeses and homemade biscuits they share pleasantries and memories about how their world has changed since their youth.

They primarily discuss resurgence of tea and its attempt to become a national drink. Ever since the Revolutionary War, loyalty and disloyalty to the drink rested on either side. If you were British, it was tea, the milkier the better. American you were a coffee man as black as it could get. Then just a few years ago a New York man put tea in a bag and sold it just as a packaging convenience but Americans in their chase for life dunked the whole bag in the way that it was not intended which sparked a new craze, one of the first ones of the new Twentieth Century.

"Speaking of tea, what did you put in this tea, Madame?" The professor glances at the brass carriage clock on the side table and then at his cup. "It's very good, not as substantial as the 'bean' but good and it is also as bad a time keeper as the clock over there, and seems to know it, causing time to secretly slip by."

"Strange that my poppa used those same words for many years but in his cup was something more rowdy and high spirited.

By the way it is the same tea you accidentally had a taste of back at the store. It is very hypnotic and gets things where you want them to go," Shirley teased.

The professor looks slightly bewildered but scoffs it off with his own interpretation.

"I do have a little English in me you know. According to Harper's their version of the language is hypnotic, our version is barely chaotic. "

The tea pot miraculously appears in her left hand before she tips a small amount of its liquid into the cup. "Warm you up a bit may I? It is unseasonable chilly isn't it? Your transportation back to Brunswick may be jeopardized....."

"I must go now then and take my leave of your hospitality!" Mallory is hesitant in his stilted reply while almost standing.

"But you didn't let me finish, what I wanted to say was I can take you in the Jackson. Haven't been to Brunswick by it all summer."

"Maybe you can, unless...." Professor suddenly remembers that his visit to Phippsburg and its real intention had not been realized. He needs more time to get his thoughts together. Maybe the answer is in the book or maybe not. "Miss Shapleigh you can share some more of those tales with me. There must be one that has more mystery."

"There is one you should hear. It is an ancient one like the last." Shirley sits retrieving the book from the mahogany side table.

ALTON

"Take from me, me merri grog
And trade it for a bole of tod
The world is combed with many
Strange things
That's why me likes me brandi
Sling..."

Alton McGonagall rose from his stool at the Four Naughts, staggered sideways through the door, and onto the road singing that verse. It was getting to midnight and Mrs. Locke had already flushed the boardwalk with six buckets of water. Now she stood motionless with the seventh one in anticipation that the stomach of her last customer might recall its night work as well. Alton noticed Mrs. Locke standing there with the bucket.

"Me lady, would you please have the courtesy to dowse this working man with a little of that...."

"Get on with you, Alton. You've had enough liquids."

He tumbled toward a brace of 'Gansett Pacers hung to a coach, and dangerously climbed up the high seat. It was then he vomited.

For twenty years Alton drove the coach for Overland Transport, riding the westward route. That's twenty years, three hundred and sixty thousand times of bouncing up and down, that's forty-six times around the earth. He figured he deserved every bowl of whiskey his head could throw back. He liked the power of being a man of travel with the ability of changing here to there, of transporting men of means closer to their money; and bringing loved ones closer to their homes. He gazed down at the helpless brood at his feet, wondering how he could untie them from the iron post.

"Here you go, Alton!" Mrs. Locke, sensing a catastrophe, reached down unleashed the reins and tossed them up and they neatly hooked on Alton's left arm.

A shout from somewhere signaled the brood of 'Gansetts to lung forward and before Locke could blink an eye, Alton and the coach disappeared into the night. It was not until Mrs. Locke picked up her pail did she notice that Alton had taken the wrong coach. Alton's was only a few feet away.

The coach barreled down High Road which overlooked the marshes and took the fork to Settlers Lane. Then it dashed across a moonlit field and waded through a restless stream which slipped from the New Meadows River.

"What's that?" Alton's eyes popped opened. He felt the reins. Instantly he knew he had the wrong coach. His reins were studded and his horses were speckled grey. Now he gripped rough hide. He pulled the reins hard, digging his butt into the wooden bench.

The horses screamed; their harnesses tightened. The universe struggled to a halt. Muffled moans and cries lurked somewhere in the dark. His heart pounded and he took a deep breath. The sounds were coming beneath. He jumped down into the deep mud that the coach's wheels churned up.

"My, God!" In front of him was the strangest carriage he had ever seen, without windows, braced with iron staves on its crown, with one door and that bolted with an iron latch. Alton easily pulled back the bolt. The moaning and the crying ceased.

He looked inside. Human shapes appeared in the darkness. He angled back to let the moonlight in. Eight

Compassion

Africans, half naked, shivering in tattered wool blankets huddled within. They smelled of a ship's devil's hole.

Alton knew well the cursed smell. When he was a teenage boy seeking adventure, he signed on to the notorious schooner Milly that rode the Atlantic looking for commerce. After a month the Milly ran down a slow Portuguese slaver and the crew forced on board seventy-five Africans heading for markets in the Azores. The Milly's captain, desiring the highest profits, set sail for the barracoons of Havana. Provisions were inadequate and the Africans, already exposed to small pox, quickly succumbed. After three days the smell became unbearable. The captain forced Alton and another man to climb down the devil's hole, pry the dead from the living and drag the lifeless bodies up to the deck. Then the two tossed the bodies, one by one, into the Atlantic. Suddenly, his eyes met the blank stare of an African about his age, bronze and lanky.

Alton remembered that the same boy smiled at him days before as he gave him water. The boy's fever was high and he offered Alton the ochre shells he wore about his neck for an additional swallow. Alton refused. There was no reason to refuse.

There was enough water to allow the crew eight cups on a daily basis, but Alton still refused. Now in an attempt to keep the limp body from sliding back into the hole, Alton grabbed its waist. In doing so, his arm slid up to the chest. There were breasts. His thumbs touched nipples. The body was of a young girl's. As his hand move upward he cut his palm on the very same necklace of ochre shells he had been offered. The young girl's ooze mixed with Alton's blood. From his arms slicked in sweat the wilted body dropped. As it did its mouth opened but

37

nothing came out. It was the silent scream he would dream about for years to come. He swore he never would go to sea again, that's why he made his living navigating land.

Alton heard shouts far in the distance. He was certain it was the agents coming for their cargo. He turned to the Africans and pleaded:

"Get out and run for your lives! They're coming!" Alton looked around for a place for the Africans to hide. Small bushes and thin ailing pine surrounded him. A cloud slipped from the moon and a beam rolled across the tide waters, revealing an island.

"There, swim there! No one goes there. It's an island lost and forgotten, cursed by the red men, they say. They'll never find you there," he shouted.

Suddenly a young woman emerged from the carriage. She was completely naked but muscles covered her thin ebony frame. Alton could make out a shape of a winged bird tattoo spread from her taunt stomach to her full breast. Her eyes blazed fury. She bounded out like a deer towards the rocks and dove into the water.

The other Africans continued to huddle in the shadows in silence. They heard the shouting too, far in the distance. Maybe they thought whoever was coming would save them from this mad man.

Mad he was, and now sober. He slammed the carriage door, bounded up the foot bar, stretched to the overhand and on to the bench. At the crack of the whip the team of horses broke out in amazing speed. The plan was to go into town, ring the church bell and make all of the townsfolk aware of the nasty transactions occurring in their midst.

The horses hit Old Center Road pounding by the rattled fences, over the Town Bridge by the cemetery, down Rope Lane and its thatched hovels, to the market where it meets Broad and southwest to the church. There they stopped. Blocking the fork in the road was Constable Bill Wells and some strangers.

"What are you up to, Alton?" The constable approached with a lantern.

"Billy, you must let them go free, you must! God help us!"

"We know that there was a mistake, Alton, but that's a pretty large order to be drinking."

"What do you mean?"

"I mean whatcha hauling 'lest it take a year for an ordinary man to finish, but for you maybe a week."

The constable held up his lantern. Alton looked behind him. He was pulling a wagon with beer barrels pyramided partially hidden beneath a huge black canvass. It only looked like a carriage.

"Are you all right, Alton?" The constable held the lantern close. He could see Alton's face had drained white.

Alton never touched a drop of spirit after that. Regardless, for a month he told his tale from his chair at the Four Naughts with a mug of mare's milk confronting him, trying to get Mrs. Locke to admit that it was a coach, not a wagon, he mistakenly took that night.

On the first anniversary of the event, which was well toasted by others, he went in search of his nightmare and was found the next morning in a barn in Harpswell asleep but drenched only in sea water. In spite of the fact that camp fires were beginning to be seen on Malaga Island, which most attributed to the reflection of fishing boats off starboard waters, Alton claimed an African

Queen resided there and he frequently visited her and when they mated halibut came out and populated the tide hole. He became the area's laughing stock, perhaps the first sober one for miles and miles.

Eventually, Overland Transport dismissed him. A year later, a son found his clothing in the alley of the general store that would one day become Scanlon's laying beside a full keg. Everyone thought that Alton had gone crazy and when his body was found it would confirm that had died of his own particular form of death, thirst. Up until the end, Alton didn't know that the Four Naught's was a meeting place for slave catchers and they transported slaves there to work in the salt works.

***

Shirley rests the book on her lap. She prepares herself for an expected onslaught of questions. When nothing comes she glances over to the professor to see if he is awake. That gesture with the fact their eyes meet seems to let loose the cork that had been figuratively placed in his mouth during the telling of the last story.

"Preposterous! Are trying to say that the former residents of that Island were the progeny of slaves, or at least a Negro slave and a hallucinating white carriage driver! An Adam and Eve of the underworld! I wonder what Darwin would say?"

"Dear, sir, have you ever heard of Lilith?"

"The myth of Adam's first wife, the woman that dared to be equal to man? Can you imagine that?"

Shirley winced and smiled to cover her disappointment, hoping that Mallory would stop right there. But he continued mockingly. ".....so Adam divorced her and God gave her earth in the divorce settlement but Adam was given another wife much more beautiful than Lilith, a woman who took his breath away, as well as paradise as a consolation prize that is, if he didn't ask any questions. What of it?"

"There are two versions of creation according to which wife you talk to, right?" She sees that he is not a total lost cause.

"So?"

"So there could be others. Thaddeus, can I call you Thaddeus? Now your football companions at school could have called you Thad. Are there two of you, Thad and Thaddeus? It's just the name. Tell me honestly could Truth be polygamous! Maybe Lilith and Eve were the same, Lilith, the biological part, the Darwin of us, and Eve, the spiritual part, the Holy Spirit. Is there only one teaching for everything? There's the Bible right, but what about the Koran or the other holy books of other civilizations?" Shirley opens the book. Her fingers slip across the pages and come to rest. She looks up at Mallory, reciting almost from memory.

CHAPTER FIVE

HUMOR

GOOD GODFREY

Children are the winters flowers
Laughter its butterflies
Good words are its gentle winds
Across its stormy skies

"My people say if you skip a pebble across a pond it becomes a ripple but if you throw a pebble high enough in the sky, it becomes a rainbow. It is biblical." Joshua, the paint person paused for a moment to suck in his upper denture plate.

"Biblical."

The children who had gathered around him waited for that. Then a whole lot of giggling circled around him like a hoop. Joshua couldn't pronounce a three syllable word without that happening. Who ever made him the island Sunday school teacher didn't know what he or she was doing.

"Biblical."

In fact no one on the island could remember if anyone made him. Joshua just liked to tell stories on Sundays. That's the day he sobered up after a long week of drinking.

"Shhhhh!" Joshua's finger touched his lips. "You laugh at Godfrey. He doesn't laugh at you."

He tried it again this time slowly.

"Bib-li-cal."

Things got quiet, only to start up again. A little whis-

42

per of a snigger soon rose to all out laughter. Joshua looked up and saw that Angus had a worm dangling from his nose, and his eyes crossed while looking at it. Of all of the eight children there, Angus was the most testing. He'd do anything to get a second look at. Once he stood on his hands upside down against the bark of a tree at a funeral. Thing was it was his momma's funeral. Joshua had the antidote for Angus, ignore him.

"We come from the mainland."

That got the children's eyes up, each looking at each other with opened mouths.

"We did?" Little Carrie asked. She had always wanted to live on the mainland.

"We were fancy, puffed up, stuck out, all ditty doodle, all whalebone no meat. We were sinners!"

"Sinners" was not a word foreign to them. It was a word used by folks in the town to describe the people on the island.

There was a rustle in the bushes. It was as slight as a breeze but it was there.

"Not enough of us were paying attention to Godfrey the Almighty and such, but one day they heard the voice of an owl say; 'Hightail yourselves up the hill where the tall cedar stands.' "

"Oooooo!" Angus interrupted flapping his arms like a dumb owl.

" 'And once you are on the hill stand under the cedar.' Some folks did, those who lived in the hills mostly," Joshua continued his eyes were wide too. "Godfrey put fire on the valley. Then He put the ice to cool the fire. After a long time the ice melted, drowned all the land except the hill tops."

"What happened to the people?" Little Carrie asked.

"Drowned."

"Even the little girls?"

"They were saved. Noah in his fishing boat comes just in time to save them."

"Why only the girls, why not everyone?" whined Walt, Jack Sumter's boy, who was usually as dumb as a door knob.

Joshua took a deep breath and just before he exhaled an answer, he saw two beady eyes in the elderberry bush below the sumac.

"Massachusetts!" It was the only swear he'd say.

His upper plate dropped again, and once again accompanied by giggles.

Joshua rose; so did the crouching shape with the biggest rump he'd ever seen.

Then Joshua sat, hoping the rump would do the same. It didn't.

The shape just moved out of the shield of the white petal flowers and stood there staring at him. It was Harold, as bald as ever in the noontime sun.

"What are you telling these children?" Harold was on the island council and he would never let anyone forget it.

"About Godfrey."

Joshua tried to cover the serpent tattoos that crawled on both arms. He forgot that Harold had seen them a thousand times before. He was now Joshua, the Sunday school teacher not Joshua, the fall down drunk who was abandoned on the island by his mates on their way to the Grand Banks. He had been four years at sea, and he had nothing to show for it but his tattooed body, his bone teeth and his love for who he called Godfrey.

Joshua was part Wawenoc and part Quebec and he

knew a lot of yarns about God even before he set sail on the whaler 'The Pearly.' There a Quaker got him and together they painted the whole Book of Genesis on a whale tooth no bigger than a hand.

"Now, Joshua, I seen those snakes a thousand times before as well as that picture of the Garden of Eden you got growing on your chest! Please don't show that to the children."

Harold cleared his voice again. "Now Joshua I'm here for a solid reason, son..."

Little Walt went up to Harold stared him in his face and said: "Mr. Harold, how do you go all around your elbow to get to your thumb when you talk? Momma says you do it all the time."

Harold cleared his voice like a preacher: "Many of us on the council are concerned that you are sousing up too much imagination with the Good Old Book. And after what I heard doing my research from that bush over there, there's more to it than just old men talking. How can you ask our children to believe that Noah's Ark landed here?"

"The facts are the facts. Noah come up in a fishing boat here, nets a flying. It's in the first Book. It's in the first Book!"

"Not here, not Malaga. It was somewhere in the Holy Land." Harold's voice raised a little, catching the attention of the children who had gone to play hide-and-seek in the elderberry bushes.

Joshua challenged: "There was a flood, water was everywhere, and how do you know where the boat landed? It's biblical." The denture plate slipped. The children missed it. They were too busy up the way looking for flowers.

"Not here, on this poor island did it land. I'm sure of that!" Harold knew that the children of the island needed education, any kind of education, spiritual or otherwise, but not Joshua's kind. He continued: "The Ark went to land somewhere in the Holy Land."

"That's just what I'm saying!" Joshua steeled, eyed his doubter like a whaler, harpoon ready to strike. "That's what I said it landed here on this holy land and I got proof!"

"Produce it you crazy old fool!" Harold's veins looked like they were about to bust out of his neck, spoiling his threadbare white collar.

Joshua turned around and pointed to the rainbow of children returning with arms stuffed with flowers.

"There it is," he shouted. "Now how did they get here, white, black, red, high yellow? How did their mommas and papas get here? How did we all get here on this island when the waters went down? Its bib...you can read it in the Bible."

You see Joshua was an ocean man and the only island he had ever seen where the people were all mixed up was Malaga.

Unable to explain the rainbow of faces in front of him, Harold just walked away muttering how real Indians didn't have to wear false teeth.

"Massachusetts!" Joshua hollered.

The upper plate fell. But instead of laughing Angus picked up a pebble and threw it high in the air. It went higher and higher and higher as if it was never going to stop.

Parishioners leaving the noon service of the First Congregational Church on the mainland saw the rainbow over Malaga, got frightened like sheep in a thunder storm and ran home.

***

Mallory laughs heartily throughout the reading. One of the pleasant things he prides himself in, is that he is probably the only one among his peers who has his original teeth. Shirley laughs too simply because Mallory does. She then clears her throat.

"Thaddeus, true that story would be amusing in fact hilarious if it wasn't true."

"True?" The professor pauses and takes a deeper breath. "What do you mean true?"

"Stayed in the air for two days. I saw it!"

Mallory's jaw drops. He heard of certain unexplained phenomena originating from the island but nothing as dramatic. A stone hanging in the air in its own orbit should have made the Portland newspapers and picked up from there to make headlines in every newspaper on the planet.

"It was up there all right but to the human eye it was locked in the corona of the sun. And when the sun lowered, a cloud cover rolled over. The one who saw it said that it seemed protected by Lucifer's wings." Shirley confesses apologetically. "It was there but I couldn't, nor could anyone who saw it prove, actually prove, it was up there.

After it falls and somebody finds it, they'll think it is an ancient stone from the Vikings or some ancient god no one could prove else wise."

"I suppose no one can prove there is a God, either. These folk tales are just folk tales aren't they? You claim you actually saw one...a miracle I mean and then you don't?" Mallory grimaces. "This seemingly educated woman saw a miracle in Midcoast Maine and she swears to it, and then she doesn't, well read another one."

"There are wagons full of miracles in the sky just look up there any day but over Malaga there are chariots full of angels or maybe as Old Scanlon would say, "Just them wicked birds!"

.

CHAPTER SIX

INTEGRITY

OLD MARY

Love is the only sugar
The body knows
That only in moderation
Its sweetness grows.

Cap in hand, blond headed Wayfarer McGonagall climbed Old Mary's granite block stairs. Her shack, flat nailed with tar paper and tarp, stood on the highest rock overlooking Casco Bay. It was only ten steps but they felt like a thousand. With his face temporarily drained of its youth and his pulse leaping, he reached the final step; he filled his lungs with sea air. Then he slowly exhaled lowering his head as if he had reached an altar.

"Is that you, Wayfarer?"

The old voice caught him at the open door: "The children are away! See that, now there is no reason why you're still wavering at the door."

Mary didn't have any children or grandchildren any longer but she had the memories of them so real most folks believed they still existed.

"Miss Mary, you're looking well this bright afternoon." He smiled. The young man could only see the tip of her nose emerging from the shadows.

"Come in? Little darling, this time there better be no excuses!"

McGonagall struggled to keep his smile. He was an honest boy brought up by his strap loving Pa. But he was about to lie again. He was about to tell a deliberate lie rehearsed over and over again in the woods. Just as he began his excuse other words dropped out of his mouth.

"Your grands are away are they? That's good, Miss Mary."

"Don't stand there son, the sea wind doesn't spare the bones."

"I can't come in, Miss Mary."

"Can't come in?"

"Yes, mum, I can't come in"

A wrinkled hand lashed out of the shadows but then slowly withdrew.

"What excuse is it this time, Wayfarer McGonagall? My grandchildren are away, my chores are done, and at this time of day yours should be too. Said, what your excuse is now?"

Wayfarer was a slow boy. He was slower than most men and boys on Malaga Island. He was taller than most. His mother had reasoned that it took extra long for his thoughts to traverse his large frame. His tongue and his lips were the last parts his thoughts would reach.

"I'll say it another way. You got a reason for not coming in, Young McGonagall?"

Now it was the time for his lie. The one he had prepared seemed not appropriate but he said it anyhow.

"I can't come in because it's, it's......"

"Come on out with it. I can take anything. I could have born you twice over if I wanted to," she mumbled.

"It's raining." He looked up at the sun asking forgiveness.

"Raining?" the old voice shrieked. The hand stuck out again this time palm up. "If it is raining, I'm Cleopatra.

50

Now I suppose if the rains you're talking about were coming down in tubs? It wouldn't make a bit of difference."

"Many folks say that you're not to make love when it's raining!"

The people of the island had many superstitions. They had come from all kinds of stock; Negro, Mic Mac, French Canadian, Cape Verdian and Stray White. The Stray Whites were the most superstitious of them all because they actually believed their lot in life could get better. Even after a long and tragic life, Old Mary was no exception. She thought a moment. Maybe the boy was right. Her mind went through all of the tales, curses and warnings she could think of. Her own recollections went back seventy years, and then add to that her mother's hundred, as well as those she shared with her long gone daughter on long nights by the fire. She had never heard of rain having anything to do with love.

"Son, the only thing you're not supposed to do when it comes to loving in the rain is to lie down buck naked in it, doing it round a patch of poison ivy!" She giggled.

"And son we ain't going to be doing nothing like that." Her voice got a little younger as she mused again. "I got a nice, wide, dry bed for us to carry out our transaction. Besides, it is not raining!"

It wasn't a transaction between her and him; it was between her and the council. It was the transaction the council made at King Connor's kitchen table. The council consisted of four islanders each representing three families on the island. The council only pretended to run things. The king had the first and last breath and mostly everything in between. He brought to the attention of the council that Wayfarer McGonagall had been seen killing sea gulls on the other side of the island. He killed them in plain view of the mainlanders of Phippsburg who sometimes peered at the doings of the people on the island with binoculars. He further reasoned if a young man was fast enough to catch sea gulls he was ready to have a woman.

The council agreed with him like it always did. Wayfarer was twenty and long overdue.

King Connor's father, the general, often said masturbation was not good for the heart, although all of the men of the island practiced it. Malaga was mostly an old widows' island and even though the widows' husbands had long evaporated into the Atlantic mist, they kept their vows.

These factors led to the employment of Miss Mary on occasion to balance certain inconveniences. Although Mary was over eighty years old, she was once a "professional" in Portland. Born on the island, she followed the 14th Maine Volunteers to Cedar Creek where her lover was killed in action.

She spent most of her thirties working in houses of ill repute on the Portland waterfront. At forty she returned to Malaga, a prodigal returning home with nothing but a whore house looking velvet trunk. Her mother stroked out shortly after that. Except for daily walks to the other side of the island where she nurtured a cluster of white temptations on a bluff, and fed the birds, she'd been in that shack for forty years.

"Come on son, days getting fretful. Sun will be dropping soon and it will be dark.

"Is that what you waiting for? Maybe I'm not cunnin' enough for you. The dark will fill in what shadows can't hide?"

"No, it's not that. It's dreams, I have dreams."

"Yes, you have dreams of a fair gal in a dancing dress, which one might turn into Cinderella."

"No it's not that."

"And she would fall into your arms."

"No it's not that"

"I must say it is a dream of every young man. Lord help us every young woman has one too! I had that dream, once I was a cunnin' young woman. Many men wanted to hold me and make love to me. They did.

"But love is nothing but taking a graceful thing, holding until it can't get way and smothering it. There was one young man; he was a student at Bowdoin down the way. He comes up here to map Tide Hole. Bare-footed I fell in so-called love with him.

"When they took him in the army I followed him all the way down to all the battles. I stayed in the supply wagons and let other soldiers do things to me. I was graceful before. I could walk the rocks at the point and twirl in the wind. Then at Cedar Creek he came to me and said he didn't love me anymore. He said I was a whore."

The blond headed boy looked at her with a blank expression. All those words didn't mean anything to him.

"And that I am!" she added. Suddenly, she realized that the man, in front of her, was younger in his mind than she thought. She decided to try another approach.

"Do you like rifles, special army ones? I got a fine picture of my friend in his uniform standing beside a rifle. He named his rifle Mary after me. If you come in, I'll show it to you."

"I can't!" Wayfarer began to back away.

"Don't go." Mary's voice changed. It rose to the octave

that comes naturally with age. "They've given me two whole dollars for this. It'll feed my grand and me for almost a month. Winter is coming and we need rubber galoshes."

"I can't."

"Dreams, what kind of excuse is that. I'll tell you what, come in and I'll be anything you want. I can be one of those sea gulls I've seen you hold so tightly on the bluff. I know what. You can come and capture me!"

Suddenly, her long neck extended out of the shadows. It held a small head with strands of hair braided around faded ribbon. Her face was bird like. Deep set eyes sunk in above dry scaly cheeks. "Please, please come in please."

But he did not. Instead the boy back downed the nave to Old Mary's sanctuary to be greeted by the joyous council finally as a man. With that lesson of life learned, the council turned the cabin into a schoolhouse where young men watched the sea gulls come and go, while waiting their own turn with Old Mary.

***

Shirley closes the book and brings it tightly to her chest.

"Look, Thaddeus, the sun's rays are about to pass the second panel of window pane. It's my poor lazy woman's sundial even though a clock is nearby, must be three."

She reaches out and takes Mallory by the hand. "I guessed you missed your transit. As I promised you I will motor you back to Brunswick and that college of yours."

"Was that old hag really just some kind of gull all along? What kind of abominations did these people practice?"

"Are you judging my poor man? How do you expect to

learn their secrets? How else can one teach chastity before one has seen the consequences of not being chaste? I found that these so-called poor degenerate people are far wiser than us. "

Mallory begins to sputter something in Latin. What falls from his lips could have been a Ph.D. dissertation on the meaning of St. Augustine's secret confessions to an African acolyte; but Shirley would have understood every word of it.

"Thaddeus, did you expect me to believe that you traveled all the way here on this day, particularly this day for something less?"

Mallory slowly stands, moves to the brass carriage clock, turns capturing her eyes and announces: "I really don't want to go Miss Shapleigh. I have to confess, owing to your pleasant company I am not ready to return."

"Good, Thaddeus, because I am not ready to take you, I like your company too. You know it is very lonely here especially since the children will not be there for me in the morning. I will miss them. My grand mere was with me for what seemed centuries, and then my beloved grand mere, who was prone to sighing, gave out her last one about a year ago and left me. My poppa before his death had been long lost in the great canyons of New York City and my brother is hiking himself to death through marriages. Thank God they are one at a time."

"And what about your mother?"

"Momma, I never knew her. I never knew that kind of devotion. When she left I was three years old. She left whispering to grand mere that she loved me and was off on a train to Boston."

"My mother was the exact opposite. She swore that I

would never find another woman to match her and went about proving it. She had a photograph of me emblazoned on a small plate hanging from a necklace she always wore. When a lady I found interesting remarked about the necklace, my mother would tell her that she had one of herself made for me and I kept it in the top drawer of my dresser. Of course, the point had been made."

"Sir, I wouldn't want that type of devotion. It is the clinging kind like the honeysuckle. Roses bloom from it before its fingers strangle the tree. The Abenaki call trees withstanding that kind of love 'people.' There is a tale about that kind of love coming from the island." Shirley slowly opens the book and reads:

CHAPTER SEVEN

GRATITUDE

Trees have their own congregation
The plants go there to pray
The grass has just one sacrament
That man will go away

Missy lost April in July, now it was four o'clock
November 15th. Missy still knelt by her poor child's
stone.

The sun was a thin string on the horizon beyond the
cedars. Most of the simple graves hid in the darkness.
Surrounding Missy were her "things"—a bowl, a chair, a
patched blanket and other odds and ends. She was a big
Negro woman. For her to get down on the earth was no
small feat, but proper mourning was no stranger to the
folks on Malaga.

People said that April was struck down by innocence.
A wolf sprang out of the shadows. It was cold and confused. April approached the wolf. She offered it a piece of
her molasses candy thinking it was a dog. It was a case
of mistaken identity. Yet after the attack, the men and
the mothers who searched the small island couldn't find
the wolf!

April was six years old and Missy's only child. She
loved dogs. Up until a year before the incident, April and
her father Enos tramped the woods, hand and hand
singing trailed by canines.

That spring right around the time of her birthday, the
constable rowed to the island to tell Missy that Enos
killed a man on a fishing boat and in retaliation the crew

tossed her husband overboard. All summer long April cried and the dogs barked with her. Then the council decreed that they stop. They did up until the time of April's death.

"Now, Missy, it's downright cold out here!" Henry Johnson put one of his wife Sadie's heavy blankets over her shoulders: "It's time to go home."

Henry was Enos' cousin. He was a small, gentle balding man with eyes that seemed to understand everything. He was on the island council. All through the summer and fall there were countless meetings about Missy's vigil as well as the barking. The 'Landers could hear the noise across the tide hole as clear as a church bell in the winter.

"Henry, thank sweet Sadie and tell her that I got to see this through."

"Sadie prays for you and April every Sunday or whenever Preacher Robert Payne can get it going."

Missy nodded in thanks.

"But the thing is Missy; the council can't make you move."

"It would take more than ten men to pick me up, not four."

"But this whole thing has become a problem. You see we think if you go home the dogs will stop barking. The whole island is riled up; nit picking at everything, that cunnin' magic of neighborly love is just slipping away."

"Why doesn't the council just 'will' the dogs to stop, like they did last year when April lost her father?"

"Well, this is something different all together. Besides all it took was a half bag of Vermont molasses candy to put the poor child's mind on other things.

This time there is trouble brewing. Yesterday when

Gratitude

Sadie went to town to sell the 'lion greens she pickled for the winter brunt, she was told if we couldn't keep the dogs from barking there'd be hell to pay for all of us on the island!"

"Who told her that?"

"The constable himself told her that."

"This is about a wolf not dogs."

Dogs ran wild on Malaga. On the shore, the men hunted dogs and took them back to the alley behind the Phippsburg jail to shoot them. On Malaga dogs ran free, but not wolves.

"There's no wolf on Malaga. We looked for it all summer. Maybe it wasn't a wolf." Henry tucked at his chin, it was the first time he had a thought like that.

"What made those bites? My baby's skin clawed away like that. And where was the constable when I lost my child. Didn't your good for nothing council asked him to come over when it happened? He was up in Aroostook County hunting somewhere?" she mocked.

"Come on, Missy, you been eating too many half cooked beans. You know those 'Landers can turn us folk on this island upside down if they want!"

"I'm not leaving here until the coat of that wolf covers my April's grave!"

Some folks said that someone from the town must have brought a wolf to the island to do mischief and then when the mischief was done, took him back.

Others said the wolf stood on two legs paws up hiding with the Standing People in the cedars when the searchers passed. To Henry, whatever the explanation it would not forestall the hundreds of residents of Phippsburg, the thousands of citizens of the State of Maine, the millions of people of the United States of

America from uprooting their island paradise because of some dogs barking.

"Let me talk to her, Hank." A quiet voice floated down from the earthen rock that sheltered the makeshift burial ground.

"Is that you, Lottie? What you doing here?" Missy squinted.

Lottie was a wisp of a person. She was barely eighty pounds and next to Missy looked like one of Missy's fingers. They were good friends up until August when she had to leave Missy's vigil to tend to her ailing husband.

"Lottie, the council fools think you can pick me up, and move me of all people?"

"Missy, you're the fool, I'm not here because of them. I'm here because of William."

"How is he? You don't have to answer that. I know he is still ailing, because if he was over it you'd be here with me on this earth waiting."

Lottie grabbed Missy's extended arm and held it.

"It is about William, he's dying."

"Dying, what is a man like him dying for?"

"He is over eighty years old, Missy."

"Then what are you doing here. Go to his bedside. Keep him from dying. Every moment you have with him you'll never regret."

"I want him to die."

Everything stopped then. The only thing that Missy could hear was Henry's chronic breathing.

"What you say?"

"I want him to die, Missy. He is in so much pain."

"Well then tell him to let go."

"He won't."

"He won't?"

60

Gratitude

"He won't because he doesn't have a grave to be buried in."

"Why not?"

"Because, you're kneeling on it, you got your things all spread out there. You got your pots and spoon on his brother Alden's grave. Good thing he's dead too because he was very particular.

"I know William's holding on until you get your justice but it's like he's standing at the door waiting for his turn. Remember, Missy, this is William's family site. Look at over there all those names are known to you. Pete was your first beau. Over there is Margie, she was a hoot, and there's Pa and his pa. The only reason why April got buried in the first place is because it was Enos' grave. William gave it to him for saving him from that shark down at the Point." Lottie's hand now rested on Missy's shoulder.

"He saved him a lot of times." Henry chimed in. "Remember that whaler that turned over. William was clean knocked out."

"And the time of the rope," Lottie added.

"What rope?"

"Enos never told you about that? Well over in the town they stretched a rope across the alley where the market is and they told William to pick up some crates. Enos was there and he saw what they were going to do. So Enos pulled on the rope and all of the crates, so the fish and the packing ice could fall on top of him. It would have killed an older man like William."

"I remember a time when they were pulling lobster...." And the stories went on and on and as they did Missy got up and picked up her belongings and half crying and half laughing at the antics of old William and her

61

husband and headed back to the row shacks, one of which was her home.

To Henry's and the council's dismay the dogs didn't stop barking. In fact they even barked louder. One night later, William died. They buried him the next day. Only then did the dogs stop barking.

Only as the wind rushed by the Standing People, William and April with Enos and the wolf came out of the shadows to stand on the rock and peer out at the lights of the town.

***

Shirley shivers and looks around to see that the door is swinging open.

"You'd never know this was the beginning of summer. If we are going to continue this we might as well go into the kitchen and get that ancient stove cranked up to do some good. I got mutton soup left over from yesterday. I only cook twice a week. Thaddeus now it's only you and me."

The Shapleigh kitchen was meant for servants to work in. In the old days four women were doing all kinds of things around the Shapleigh house that is after their own houses were seen to and their husband's traps caught up and hanging. Now they are working in the hotels and cottages for the summer folk who are paying much more. The room has high ceilings walled with green tile. The table stretches endlessly toward a huge cabinet where most of the items on the table should have belonged. All sorts of pots, pans, dishes, cups, utensils, containers, canisters congregate at that end. On the near end are items one would not expect to see on a kitchen table, writing implements, old newspapers, sewing machine parts, a garden spade, a knitting kit, an odd

62

piece of clothing. It is obvious Shirley lives at that end when not occupied with sleeping.

Against the wall sits an ancient Mott stove lingering beside a tub of coal. Its cylindrical oven looks like a midget locomotive off its track. Sitting on its cast iron top is a friendly looking pot waiting to be brought to life. Shirley sees to it. The professor finds the mutton soup pleasing. He has never tasted anything like it particularly the sharp bite of curry. When Shirley was younger her father engaged the services of an East Indian cook who wooed his employers with exotic odors before he stole from them.

In a hasty exit the cook left his recipe book. So her father passed it along to her with the Jackson automobile and the decaying house.

"There is something you must clarify for me Miss Shapleigh." Mallory dunks a hunk of black seed bread into the soup.

"You can call me Shirley, now that you've seen the worst of me," she says with a hand indicating the chaotic kitchen table with certain panache.

"In the last tale you indicated that there was a murder, the little girl's father?"

"Enos, yes that was a sad affair, it happened before I returned to Phippsburg. The county got riled up about Negroes running wild on the island and what township, Phippsburg or Harpswell, had the responsibility to clean things up. The truth was no one would. My grand mere used to say that 'murder' was the only word in Webster's Bible that caused the weak to have hope. Her thumb finds a page in the book. "It is explained in the following tale, if anything like injustice can be explained that is."

CHAPTER EIGHT

TRUST

THE ISLAND YONDER

These days
Trust is an invisible thing,
(Except on bridges.)
Yet even then,
We don't know if
God is at the other end.

The meaning of life suddenly occurred to Enos. He laid the oars down onto the bottom of Mr. Anderson's dory *Joanne* and opted to float on what was left of the reflection of the late afternoon sky.

"Boy, what are you up to?" Mr. Anderson looked back and saw that Enos had quit.

The craggy Phippsburg man continued to pull himself toward the sunset in his beloved *Amy.* Both boats were stuffed with herring. Both had been pushing down the New Meadow to make it to the dock where a wagon was waiting to take their load to Portland for the morning market. Now Enos was just bobbing up and down with the pulse of the mixing tide.

"Enos, what's gotten into you? Get going!" Enos was in his employ for the moment. All the men from Malaga hired out on a temporary basis.

"Get going, you bastard!" Mr. Anderson's voice trailed as the distance between them increased. Then it suddenly occurred to Mr. Anderson that Enos might be planning to steal his catch. He usually only hired men from the island with some white ancestry.

This time was the exception. He needed nearly all the profit from this trip to buy his ailing wife the medicine prescribed by a Brunswick doctor. He had found that the blacker the skin of a man from the island the least wages he would settle for. Since Enos' black head was blacker than most of the men who stood in line earlier that morning, he thought Enos would settle only for a mere portion of the catch. Now Mr. Anderson thought that Enos wanted all of it, at least the share he pulled in. This caused the fifty-five year old white man to muscle in his oars, reach in his inner pocket and draw out a revolver. Then balancing himself he shot at Enos.

Enos didn't budge. He just let the movement of the water determine the outcome. Anderson aimed again. This time instead of a black man sitting in a boat he saw his wife, her head weighted on a yellow encrusted pillow, fever bathing her forehead, eyes so sunken their lids cracked. He pulled the trigger. When he couldn't steady himself he lost his balance and fell into the water. Most Maine fishermen can't swim very well.

Mad as all get out, Anderson struggled to free himself from the tow where New Meadows River met Casco Bay. At first he felt hands pulling him down then he felt hands pulling him up.

"Are you okay, Mr. Anderson?"

As Anderson's eyes popped open he could see the strong Negro face looking down on him.

"God?"

"No, it just Enos, but wouldn't it be something if I was."

"Are you going to kill me?"

"Kill you? Why would I do that?"

65

"So you can have all the catch you want."

"Why would I want that?"

"So you can have my catch." Anderson raised his head and looked toward his dory *Amy*.

It was upside down, its contents reclaimed by the waters.

"Mr. Anderson, I don't want your catch!"

"You're not going to steal it?" Mr. Anderson questioned.

"Steal it?" Enos laughed.

"Then why did you stop rowing?"

"I know the meaning of life, now. Took me sixty-three years but now I do."

"What are you talking about?"

"Like these here herring. You know sir, how you put up the weirs late at night, lash the nets to it, stake it out. When we come to it this morning it was so stuffed a pregnant woman could give it birth. Everything was right with the earth, the sky was blue, sun warm on my face then you began shouting orders, 'Do this, do that' things changed. It got darker and colder even with the sun blazing down. And then it happened right where we were roping them in, I saw one of them herring jump up, look at me then wiggle back into the water.

Of all the Bible talking talk I have heard in my life, it came down not to love, goodness, respecting others, even praising God Almighty, it came down to freedom."

"Boy, you almost ruined our lives for that?" Anderson shivered.

"Why not, I doubt you even got it!"

"Freedom, I have it. Nobody tells me what to do or what to say! I am my own man, not like you people!"

Enos just stared at the hunched over, trembling

soaked body. He had never seen a white man so beaten before. Anderson sensed this. He bundled himself trying to keep this frailty unexposed. Not for his sake, not under these circumstances, but for the sake of his race. He felt completely at the mercy of the man in front of him and he knew Enos was right, freedom he had little of. It was the first time he realized it. That's why he quit his job at the processing plant before the "Frenchies" came in and found a way to replace him. So was it the same for his house. It was the same one he lived since his birth, the one with the same tobacco stains his great grandfather made spitting on the hallway wallpaper. It was a house that grew smaller each decade so that the people in it struggled to be free.

Most of all, it was the net of his marriage. He had been married to Joanne for twenty years. All that was left was the husk. Now she positioned herself as such in their bed on the second floor of the family house. He had long ago found Amy, the Irish girl who worked in the bakery. He wedded her every time their palms touched. Joanne had sensed the relationship and perhaps the knowledge of it led to her illness.

Who was to say; only time would tell? It was the first time he realized that he didn't have as much freedom as he thought.

"You people know nothing of freedom, I can't blame you though. You never had much of it. But now come to think of it you've got that island, yonder."

Both men could see the gas lights of the town they floated toward. They also could see the shadow of trees on the island that seemed to grow from the sea beyond it.

"Yes, sir, we got paradise." Enos thought of his wife

Missy and girl April standing on the rock in the wind waiting for him to come home. Then he thought of their hunger. His girl had a little worn sweater to keep her from the wind. He thought of his wife wrapped in anything she could find, her bare feet curving around the uneven granite.

"Yes, sir, we got paradise, but no freedom."

It was Enos' last words as he toppled into the bay; the water was too black to see the crimson halo spreading around him.

He didn't kill a man! Anderson reasoned. He later would tell the constable the man tried to steal his catch. But he knew deep inside of him for the rest of the nights of his life that Enos had stolen something much more.

***

After a pleasant meal Mallory usually plunges his deep red pipe through his lips and draws, but the astonishing tale he has just heard and the respect he has for his equally astonishing hostess keeps his fingers away from the pipe and pouch hidden in his inside pocket. Shirley receives his compliments well, noticing her guest's silent belch as a man's true sign of gratitude. This time she follows him into the parlor and watches as he lowers himself on to the blue velvet divan right in the same spot her father use to sink.

She giggles. Mallory looks up and realizes that he sat before his hostess is able to do so. Yet he is the guest but she is the woman. He begins to rise but she signals him not to. Etiquette was always confusing to him.

"After that last tale all I felt like doing was collapsing. Do you mind if I indulge in my only vice, I have so few, Madame?"

Trust

"Let me guess, Viola tobacco! It's only natural. It's been so long that it might put the draperies in shock! Papa smoked there often, when he was around, from that very spot. Magnetism."

Mallory takes out his kit. Pinching out the tobacco he stuffs it into the briar bowl. Gracing his lips with the stem, then anchoring his jaw on it as he pulls a tin box from his vest, then he takes out the match stick to strike, spark and ignite. A plume of smoke curls upward toward the fluted ceiling.

"How did you come about these tales anyhow Miss Shapleigh?" Mallory asks with a modicum of suspicion.

"It's Shirley, call me Shirley, Thaddeus! And as I told you I found this book one morning on my table at the school."

"The tales were in them?"

"Yes, not all of them, every month at least not a month went by when another one was added."

Mallory draws in and expels a cloud of smoke resembling a character in one of Arthur Conan Doyle's short stories.

"You're sounding very unpleasant, my friend, at least I thought you were, not unpleasant that is, but my friend!" She approaches him standing as if straddling her words. "What are you insinuating, sir?"

"First you tell me these extraordinary stories, ranging from murder to miracles written so carefully that they could have appeared in the Monthly, by different authors no doubt, different styles, pacing. Remember I am a college professor and make my living disclosing adolescent literary hoaxes." Mallory stands and faces her. She holds her gaze, so does Mallory. She has never been this close to the breath of a man, Doctor Abraham Hoffman D.O.

69

not counting. She sees now what they are all talking about. Forty years is a long time coming.

Attraction can not only be an explosion but a gentle breeze of breath albeit this one with a hint of Prince Albert mixture and curry. Shirley can't keep up the façade; she must either kiss him or hit him. She does what any woman of her background and breeding would do. She swings around and goes to the side table to see if the water is hot enough for tea.

"As I see it sir, the stories were meant for one thing." She continues. "To be read to the children I tended to. It was a part of their history just as like over on Topsham Mrs. Thingamabob reads the stories from U. S. history every morning which are mostly about wars. The tales in our book are about goodness and how to attain it. There are some I don't read to them. I think they are primarily meant for me." Shirley brightens a bit and notices that Mallory is still standing puffing away like her father used to do while waiting for one of his children's confessions. She laughs because he rarely got one.

"As for the difference in the writing you got me there just like the appearances. These are strange as well as wonderful people, full of surprises. Like one afternoon I was going over the necessities of passable penmanship with a seven year old who would rather communicate in Egyptian hieroglyphics when I looked down on the workbook I thought he was doodling in and I saw that he had just completed a quote from Oscar Wilde: *The true mystery of the world is in the visible not the invisible.*"

"You read it! What did the boy say? What was his explanation; surely you got to the bottom of it?" Mallory's pipe almost fell from its perch.

"Say what? You want an explanation? You think he

was the one who was planting the stories in the book? Ridiculous, like they say around here that boy was 'nummer than a hack.' And even if he was behind it or knew something about it and shared it with strangers there would be consequences. I'm going to get more of that heated water in the kitchen and when I come back, I'm going to read you a tale from the book pertaining to just that."

CHAPTER NINE

HONESTY

THE FAR AWAYERS

The people pulled in the tide
And covered up the continent
And when the night came
They looked for a place to rest
They wondered too late
Where the cities went

"So this is Nigger Island!" exclaimed the stranger.

The sun had past its high point and was about to roll down. It was a little after two and the tide had scampered back as far as it could go. Perhaps it knew that Jack Sumter would be coming, dragging behind him Walt, his boy, struggling to carry enough buckets to hold at least four "pecks" of clams.

"Only an old man and a boy coming," replied the other stranger.

A tight breeze wrapped the cove. Fall was falling fast on Malaga. The sumac was almost out of colors, and parts of the flats had gone from textured black to reddish ore. The summer was rusting out and the squawk of the last heron was warning.

Jack spotted the two curiously dressed white men in the distance. They were in pullover bib shirts and shawl collared silk vests, rubber booted up to their thighs and stuck deep in the mud.

"Don't look like diggers to me."

"Far away folks, looks like, Pa." Walt dropped his

buckets.

Jack knew most of the men who at times dug on nearby Bear Island. Surf clams were there "aplenty" and practically no green crabs prowled the sands looking for clam necks to snap. Besides nobody from the mainland forked Malaga's flat for fear the clams were poisoned. The men in front of them were not diggers.

The taller man approached him with his hand extended.

"Mister Hanley, here!"

He had never been asked to shake hands with a white man in gloves before. So he kept his arms dangling to his side, fork in his belt.

"Usually, I take them off but it's so. You know. Or do you?"

"Those folk don't shake hands, sir?" The second man's eyes met Jack's. "Do you boy?" When Jack didn't look away, or look down like coloreds always did, the man was a bit bewildered.

"Don't aggravate him, Lester. Coming upon us like this must be unnerving. After all, this is their island." The man turned to Walt. "Is he your son?"

Jack nodded and placed a hand on top of Walt's head, who was cowering beside him.

"Maybe they don't speak English, sir?"

"Rubbish!"

Lester obviously was an aide of some kind to Hanley. He was cruder than Hanley. He looked like one of those angular men who sat around Scanlon's General Store jiving whoever walked in. He did dress better, but his silk vest didn't fit, buttons struggling at the chest, and his shirt opened at the top obviously for air.

Jack had seen his type sitting on top of carriages in

Brunswick, carting around men like Hanley and shouting down obscenities to black men like him. "I say rubbish Lester because everyone speaks the King's English."

"These people aren't people, sir, they're natives." Lester resumed his stare.

Haney was a different sort. Mattie, Williams' wife, would call him "lovely." His raven black hair, neatly cut, framed his well portioned face. His furrowed brow seemed to be a Rosetta Stone of taste, although one had to wonder what knowledge was resting beneath.

"Deaf and dumb, they got homes for people like these!" Lester waved his palm in front of Jack several times, but Jack didn't blink. "And they're blind, too!"

Jack was in a trance. Hanley's paisley collar and tie wove strange patterns across his eyes. Rain drops in green forests, chimeras between hibiscus blooms; he had never seen such shapes before. All of this was highlighted by the sun which escaped a cloud and hit upon what seemed to be a golden key dangling from Hanley's neck. It was solid brass and its shaft fluted to the butterfly wing bow.

There was a graceful mystery about it.

"My friend, let's get down to the point and skip social formalities. I want to buy your island. The men in the town, when I made them aware that I was looking to buy a fishing island suggested I come over here and talk to you."

"Mister, this place doesn't belong to a miserable man like him, it belongs to the king." Walt just spoke up like he always did because most folks thought he was dumber than a door knob, and wouldn't listen to anything he had to say anyhow.

"King, they are backwards, Lester!" Hanley turned to

the boy and then to Jack. "You poor fellows haven't you heard of the Aroostook War? This island is yours now. How much are you asking?"

The king Walt referred to was King Conners who claimed his father had a deed to the island and misplaced it when he was feeding the pigs.

Then Lester noticed how intently Jack was staring at his employer's key. He whispered something in Hanley's ear which brought a wide smile to both their lips.

"We trade. Me-give-you-key for island!" Hanley said haltingly in his best Indian talk, straight from James Fenimore Cooper's, *The Last of the Mohicans.* Lester reminded his employer that white men had traded similar trinkets in the past for more valuable land; the island of Manhattan for one. Slowly Hanley removed the key chain from his neck. The key still caught the glint of the sun. Jack finally fingered it.

Perhaps the key was to a treasure chest hidden in a hidden cave somewhere on the mainland, or to a room at the top of the stairs of a fine hotel or yet again maybe it was the key to happiness, Jack laughed to himself.

Lester produced a document from his vest pocket. They had come prepared. All summer the duo traveled up and down the Maine and New Hampshire coast looking at real estate. A savvy banker told them that Casco Bay fishing had a reputation, especially where the New Meadow flowed.

"Sign here and this key is yours." Hanley motioned.

Now Jack never had to sign anything in all of his fifty years. He was not a writing man. An agreement to him just meant a smile and a nod. Lester took out a small bottle of ink and a pen. He anointed the pen tip and handed it to Hanley. He ceremoniously cradled the document on his right arm so that Hanley could scrawl his name. Finally, Hanley handed the pen to Jack. In what he perceived as sign language, he motioned to the key and then down to the mud flat where they stood.

Jack reasoned that if Hanley was trading his key for that piece of mud flat and he didn't accept it, he was no Maine boy. Jack eagerly grabbed the pen and signed the document.

John Forester Sumter

The signature was not an "X" or crudely done. It was graceful scrawl and showed the intelligence and patience of an enlightened man. Hanley and Lester were astonished. If they hadn't seen Jack's own hand move across the signature line of the contract they would have dismissed it as an illusion. Things were not what they seemed. Now the two white men looked around the cove and saw dead things: gnarled roots, entangled in seaweed, dotted the shore line. Fire seemed to have singed the scrub pine.

The smell of decaying fish permeated the air. Above, black birds circled, one wing was enough at times to block out the sun.

"What happened to this place? Let's get of here," shouted Hanley.

In fear that they were about to trade for what they perceived as Hell, Hanley tore up the document and pulling Lester by his arm waded through the mud to the other side of a protruding rock where their dory waited. Soon they were out of sight.

It was only when they arrived at the guest house did they remember the key. They dropped it in the water, that's what they told Mrs. Anderson before she gave them another one.

"That's what you get for going to that wicked island!" She couldn't help to say.

Two weeks later in search for an island to acquire, the pair crashed into Vinal Haven and a group of lobster adventurers craftier than they were. They were last seen in an old Jersey Skiff passing Machias Bay headed out to who knows where in the open sea.

As for Jack and his son, the rest of the afternoon went well. They raked more pecks and shared them with all of the families.

Jack gave the key to Walt who talked about the encounter for weeks. Everybody knew that he was dumber than a door knob but he wasn't a fibber. The council eventually got hold of the key. And in the middle of night, if the room in the boarding house was not occupied, part of the room if not all of it, was put to good use.

**

After the last tale Mallory and Shirley arrange themselves at either end on the divan. They are both holding mugs, but in Mallory's other hand he holds his pipe and in Shirley's other hand she grasps the book. The tea is huskier than Mallory wants it to be. He grimaces. A tea drinker he is not, tea leaves sit too long in their brew. Coffee's anger is boiled out of it.

"Here we are like an old married couple."

"Hardly, Madame!" Mallory adjusts his collar.

"Think about it we just met this afternoon and we are now arguing about reality. These are modern times."

"What do you mean?"

"Perception, like you said where you see murder and I see magic. Or like in the latter story where Hanley and his companion saw hell, Enos, the real hero in the former story saw paradise."

"Enos was the victim, I say." The professor lowered his mug.

"More tea, Thaddeus?"

"Do you have any coffee, at all? I beg of you tea is not my cup of ......you know what I mean!"

"I am sorry, we have none, but I am pleased that all this time you satisfied yourself with what I offered you. It shows that you have character which is a real rarity out here."

"Out here?"

"Yes, out here as compared to the people on the island. They have learned patience, fortitude and integrity. If they have a task they do it and complete it. They don't whine and make excuses. It is the secret to survival. I hope you're ready for another story?"

CHAPTER TEN

FORTITUDE

DIGGERS

The young have no burden
Save their age,
Yet they carry it everywhere
They go.

"Ooooha....Oooooha...Oooooha!" Goodboy grunted.

Angus and Prince hunkered down in the sea grass that guarded the sand dune patch at the peak on Bear Island. An October sun crawled slowly in the distance like a beetle on the sky.

Ooooooha...Ooooha....Ooooha!"

On the beach Goodboy dug feverishly for steamers as if his life depended upon it. He looked like some worm in the mud with a hump on it trying to find its way to Kingdom Come. Sometimes he'd come up with a broken plate or cup. Most times he came up with a clam, which was so terrified in its shell you could almost hear it scream.

"Look at him go!" Prince shook his head in amazement.

"Momma once told me he was born that way. He was born to dig. If you're born to dig that's what you do." Angus replied with more than just jealousy but something tinged with hate.

Goodboy was his half-brother and even though Goodboy was stricken with ugliness, the real deep kind, he was always the apple of his mother's eye. When Angus came along who was a lot prettier, her focus didn't change. Goodboy's pa was unknown. Like the Jesus, it was a miracle Goodboy came. He was all twisted up so that when the birth cord got straightened, it was so long the girls could have played jump rope. His humpback had hair on it so when he came out they thought he was a twin.

Even though when Angus was a bundled up child, Goodboy was the one who got all of her attention. Every morning his mother rubbed a salve made from dry moss, spit and a grubby root on his hump back until it was practically purple.

It was "Goodboy this" and "Goodboy that," she'd coo. Angus bawled so much that whoever came by had to give him a tit or thumb to suck on. When it came to Agnus' poppa, everybody knew who he was. He was one of the ones who came in and out with the tide. As soon as the mackerel was hauled in and Portland jails washed out, he would be showing up in a dingy on the north side inlet beneath the bench drunk beside an oar. Soon he would sober up and wander around to find a girl to capture with his stories and smile. It was a late August night when he caught Angus' momma and had his way with her. A couple of hours later Goodboy stumbled upon them. They could have found Angus' Pa in China for he was found deep in a hole turned inside out.

That's why folks on the island sometimes called Angus "orphan boy" even before his momma crossed over to the River Jordan's other side.

Many a night he dreamed that his half-brother had died too, but to no avail, in the dream another brother that looked just like Goodboy would always climb out of the top of his hump ready to do the morning's digging.

"Thump! Thump!"

"Hear that?" Prince, put his head flat to the ground to listen for footsteps.

A wasp threatened to come down and give away the boys' position but decided not to.

Angus' ear flattened to the dirt too. He couldn't hear a thing just the faint sound of Goodboy digging in his other ear.

"Don't hear nothing!"

"They say when he comes, the whole earth shakes. The piper birds flit out like bees and the flowers wilt backwards because of the smell." Angus boasted like he knew something but he didn't.

Although Bear Island was the next island over from Malaga, the boys were not supposed to have been there. But the flats on Malaga were getting to be barren of clams. There was enough star fish on them to stud the night sky. Island folk said that Bear Island belonged to a big bear or something that looked just like one, all they knew was it wore a red plaid shirt. And whatever it was, only let townspeople dig there because they paid it money. The people from Malaga didn't like whatever it was, like the townspeople didn't like them.

Then Angus rested his chin on his closed fist and watched his brother work.

Angus in a way admired his brother's body. His body molded to the task. He worked with such ease. All he could see then was joy in beads dripping from his forehead.

"Ooooha....Oooooha...Oooooha!"

"Doesn't he ever get bushed out?" Prince scooted over on his back, "I am."

81

Usually stretching out on sea grass is not like stretching out on meadow grass. On sea grass the sand fleas just eat you up. Prince might as well have been on his own bed, which was old stale hay filled with another kind of bug.

Angus was his best friend, but they were not two peas in a pod either. Prince was long legged and as black as a coal stove and Angus was short, freckled with wild fiery red hair and sun tanned skin. Angus was always going; Prince wasn't.

On the island it was the custom for everyone to take turns clamming; sharing was a necessary way of living. Everyone shared equally. Old Gus Matthews got the left-overs to process in his fish shack. He mixed them with worms and sold it as bait. What he got from the sale provided cow milk for all. That was his contribution. Prince's family was among the latest families to come to Malaga. His grandparents were from Georgia and had been slaves.

They fled up north in the vacuum General Sherman left, eking out a living for many years in Philadelphia, Boston and then to Portland. Prince's folks pulled corn stalks and bagged cotton when they were young. By the 1880's their palms had become soft from slacking and begging.

Although Prince was born on Malaga he inherited some of his parent's inclinations to prepare and not acquire. So when it came time for him to "dig the clams" he would ask Angus and his brother Goodboy to help him. He and Angus would be the lookouts. Goodboy would do the work.

"Ooooha....Oooooha...Oooooha!" Goodboy would holler.

Fortitude

"Zzzzzeeeee...up, Zzzzzeeee, sup.   Just like that,
Prince fell asleep. That's when the wasp which had been
hovering above him all along decided to get hungry. It
dived and stung Prince, right in the middle of his forehead. He looked like an Indian Maharaja with a ruby
stuck between his eyes. Prince jumped up, and let out a
scream. People probably heard it all the way down Casco
Bay. At first Prince tried to run all the way down Casco
Bay, then remembering that it was all water, ran back on
the beach in the opposite direction.

Through all of it Goodboy kept digging. Angus tried
to run after his friend. Slipping on a shell mound, he fell
flat on the sandy dirt. That's when he heard the thump-
ing.

"Thump ...Thump....Thump!"

At first he thought it was Goodboy's rake pounding
into the mud, then he thought it was own heart echoing
in his ear. Then he realized it was Prince running all the
way back.

"He's coming! He's coming!" Prince ran right by him
and into a nearby cluster of boulders.

Angus looked to the right and saw the whole forest
moving.

"Come on Angus get your brother and get your feet
moving! We can get to the skiff from the other side of
these rocks!" Prince shouted.

Angus looked at his brother who believe it or not was
still digging. But the wide smile that routinely was on
Goodboy's face was gone.

"Ooooha....Oooooha...Oooooha!"

He rushed to Goodboy and tried to pull him away and
all he was able to do was to hold down the rake. Blood
soaked the handle and he looked up and saw the pain in

his brother's face. The palms and fingers of his hand had stiffened. Angus could almost see pain leaking through the raw flesh. All this time he thought that Goodboy was born to dig. Yes, the truth was Goodboy's body was no more born to dig than he was. It went further back to the stew that puts together the human soul.

Somehow Angus' older big brother knew and his head looked up in expectation. Angus picked up the bloodied rake and faced what was coming through the thicket.

It was just like the sun coming out of a grey unwanted cloud, he came. He could have been a god in the olden days. If he stood who knows how tall he would be. He was near seven feet bent over. A brown wood like beard meshed across his face hiding most of his features, except his eyes, small like an ordinary man's but fiery enough to pierce through the wild brows above them. How he ever got a shirt to fit him who knows but it was red plaid and the description of the rest of his clothing, like belt, pants and shoes was blinded in the fear of seeing what hung above them. As he turned a most starling thing happened, Angus saw burdened on the giant's back was a hump so immense tree branches dangled from it and the remains of a birds nest floated off. The giant approached Goodboy and looked down. Goodboy looked up and he curiously started to dig again.

"Ooooha....Oooooha...Oooooha!"

The monster squatted down to the earth trembling, and with his gigantic hand dug with him.

"OOOOOOOHA.......OOOOOHA........OOOOOHA!"

To save the sanity of villagers in the surrounding areas and the doubters of what they knew of reality, God sent a thunderstorm so loud it was convincing. The fishing boats up in the Grand Banks waited for retribution.

Fortitude

Surprisingly, it was Prince who heroically dragged Angus down to the raft and oared through the shafts of lighting and lash of waves.

The next week some council members approached Angus and inquired about the whereabouts of his half brother. They planned to increase the clam rations for the coming holiday.

Angus told them that his brother was up and about but since everyone was so used to him and the way he looked he went around unnoticed like he always wanted to be. True to Angus' word, ten baskets of clams were found the next evening on old Gus' makeshift pier waiting to be distributed.

For a whole year Angus and Prince had no problem getting all the clams they wanted until the day they sneaked to the beach on Bear Island and nothing was there waiting for them. That was when the boys learned how to dig clams themselves. The whereabouts of Goodboy became a real concern on Malaga until the rumor got out that he had went West to dig for clams where no one else could, in the middle of the desert.

By spring next, the council tracked him down and got him to come back to the island for a very special task.

Shirley closes the book and sighs dramatically.

"Well, well, finish the tale!" Mallory is beside himself.

"I am not permitted to tell that part of the tale, unless," cautions Shirley.

"Unless...?"

"I think....." She reopens the book and carefully thumbs away the pages until her palm rests.

"I read on!"

CHAPTER ELEVEN

LOVE

THE PARASOL

Mothers
Are flowers
Unloosed to give
Birth
In the heart

"Hush!"

Lydia Herschel-Brown was so thin you could spit through her, and she was getting thinner every day. There was no doubt in anybody's mind that one day she would set like the sun was trying to do beyond her. She had only two wishes left in her life. One was to see Africa with her own eyes. There she sat, strapped in her wheel chair on Mr. Phillip's white launch with a pair of opera glasses gazing at Maine's version of Africa.

Her mother and her nurse Liz surrounded her with peppermint colored parasols. Her husband Michael, sporting a small Prince Albert beard and one of those straw woven hats straight from France, held her hand. It would have been a perfect study if it was on the Seine or at least the Kennebec, but not on the old basin which cupped Malaga. They looked like some Bangor photographer had told them to hold their breaths then went out for a beer. That's how they floated on the basin that late summer afternoon.

"What a dreadful pity we didn't go to the Columbian Exposition, Lydia," Michael commented, knowing that

Love

Lydia was too ill to go to Portland let alone Chicago. "I understand they installed an authentic African village with pygmies running around in the most unspeakable state."

"Hush!" Lydia spotted a weathered fish shack jutting up from the beach. A slight smile curved beneath her opera glasses. Everything was so still, as Brunswick people would say, "Even the water obliged,"

"Look dead to me." Old Gus said to Little Girl as he peered out at them through the knot hole he never got around to fixing on the port side of his fish shack. *Worse than a bunch of widows at a dance!*

Little Girl was only four years old and had the brightest red hair you ever want to see. She wouldn't have understood what he was saying if she could. He went back to stripping down the large haddock on the bench in front of him. People said of Old Gus that he was a queer man who always did good. He was dawn black with skin as thick as oak bark. He had a fisherman's eyes and head. He was used to seeing people from the mainland floating up in a skiff, or a dingy to take a glimpse of the island. He wasn't used to seeing a launch spending the whole afternoon doing it.

Lydia coughed. Suddenly everything on the boat came alive. Parasols closed. Shawls draped over her shoulders. Handkerchiefs covered faces. Hands reached for the medicine bottle in a bag at the bottom of the boat.

"Michael, we should return before sun sets. She needs rest." Lydia's mother cautioned.

"Mother, we can't go now. The natives haven't come out yet. We don't know if she's with them or not. "

All of Lydia's life she had been in love with Africa. Not Africa the place but Africa the dream. She dreamt of animals that came from fairytales. She dreamt of jungles that came from *Harper's Illustrated.* She dreamt of a child of Africa that came from her desire to do "good" in the world. That was her second wish.

She wanted a child to hold. She had been only married a year before she got lung fever. Her husband Michael wasn't the aggressive kind. While waltzing even after their engagement he refrained from touching her waist without a glove. And things of the bedroom, well we must leave those matters in there, as Mrs. Herschel advised, where they belong.

Little Girl was the island's orphan. The council tried to match her up with Missy after she lost her girl April, but Missy still boarded April in her heart. The council then asked Mattie. She had an empty cot and a place at her table.

She claimed she was too old to take on the child. Even Mother Washington didn't think it was feasible to raise a girl along with a gaggle of boys in a one room shack. Family after family regretfully refused to harbor her. Part of the reason was because no one knew who her parents were. The real reason was how she arrived on the island.

Old Gus found Little Girl alone in a row boat beached on Malaga sand. She was bundled in a crate like Moses on the river Nile. No one knew where she came from, just that she wasn't mulatto. She had been with Old Gus ever since. Little Girl went a whole summer and a winter without saying a word. That was all right because folks said Old Gus babbled enough for both of them.

"Look at them out there; you'd think that they'd never seen a fish house before." The old man picked Little Girl up in both arms so she could see for herself. All she could see were the parasols that seemed to float by themselves on the water. They reminded her of the candy that Old Gus had traded for a month before.

"Lydia, haven't you had enough of this?" The back of Mrs. Herschel's hand rested on her daughter's forehead. Lydia pushed it away because it blocked her view of the fish house. When not engaged in her activities with the Women's Christian Temperance Union Mrs. Herschel life centered on the well being of her daughter. Her world had been one of filigree and lace. Germans by stock, they were shipbuilders from Waldoboro. Lydia grew up dining at a dinner table with a bronze model of a five mast schooner sitting smack in the middle of it. But when she stood at her bay windows to watch the construction of her father's ships her mother pulled the drapes.

"Darling, I don't think we are ever going to see anything, remarked Michael as he left the tableaux of parasols. He balanced himself across the redwood deck to the steam boiler where Mr. Phillip's impatient deck boy stood by with a watchful eye for the signal to depart.

"We'll see her. She was in my dream!" Lydia replied to her husband as she refocused her opera glasses on the barnacle covered fish shack. "She was in my dream."

"They are still looking at us. I wonder if they want to buy some of them steamers." Old Gus stooped to a basket filled with clams. The girl watched him intently. Old Gus knew that he wouldn't be able to keep Little Girl for long. Think of it, she lived in a place where an old queer man gutted and flushed fish; an old queer who never had a woman let alone a child to care for. Some of the women thought the arrangement was outrageous even though they were not willing to take her in.

The council contemplated sending her back to the

mainland so the churches of the town would see fit to do what they all do in such circumstances. Holding the basket high, he angrily kicked the door open.

Hearts stopped on the launch. Parasols dropped. Breasts clutched. Opera glasses fell. The sight of the basket of clams above boots emerging from a rickety door even startled Mr. Phillip's deck boy who must have seen the combination hundreds of times.

The boy instantly sounded the horn.

When Old Gus walked through the doorway, Little Girl followed.

Through her opera glasses, Lydia saw a red frizzy haired, wide nosed, thin-lipped girl with blue eyes and brown arms reaching out toward her.

She tried to get up from her wheelchair. She begged the deck boy to bring the launch closer to the beach, but at Michael's insistence the launch moved in the opposite direction.

In the confusion a parasol fell overboard. Little Girl, who eyed something new to play with, ran into the water after it.

Hearing the horn, the islanders rushed to the knoll overlooking the beach. Once there they saw the launch slip away. Then they saw the little girl in the water. Old Gus, who was still intent on selling his steamers, didn't notice her at first but when he did he looked like Moby Dick pushing aside the Atlantic to get to her.

Missy, followed by Mattie, rushed down the small hill as if yelling could save anyone. Old Gus got the little one and soaked to the bone handed Little Girl to Missy for that motherly curing. She held the child so tight in her ample breast the action pushed open her heart.

"Do you think they tried to steal her?" Mattie said to

Love

Old Gus, remembering the tales of the days when slave catchers scoured Maine looking for human property.

"Might have, they looked wicked weird to me. They wanted something. Now what do we have to give?"

Quickly the islanders arrived on the beach and hugged and kissed Little Girl as if they never seen her before.

They shook hands with Old Gus who they always thought was someone special but never had the opportunity to express it.

When the islanders surrounded Missy to congratulate her, the orphan tumbled unnoticed underneath her grasp and ran to the drifting peppermint parasol beckoning to her from the swell. As quickly as the sun skedaddles after it reaches the horizon, the small red headed girl slipped beneath the waters.

Although the launch was not that far away, the sailing party watched the horror through their opera glasses.

"Do you think the little girl will be all right? Maybe we should notify the constable, or someone." Mrs. Herschel asked her son-in-law.

"Too late, Mother Herschel, she's gone." Michael sighed as one does at the end of a well produced opera.

But Lydia's reaction was different. Nurse Liz testified at the hearing that she thought she saw Lydia unleash the restraint that secured her chair to a rail and push herself off the deck.

They found the chair the next day, Lydia was not in it. Two weeks later a storm swept in like a November broom and blew up drift wood and roots and all kind of things to a shape on top of Mary's rise. To Old Gus who could see it from his shack, it resembles a mother and a child. And to the folk on the mainland—those who had binoculars,—it looked like what it was, a mystery.

At that point Shirley carefully puts her book down, turns around and looks intently at the entrance to the kitchen as if she is expecting someone to enter like her memory coming in.

She inhales deeply and returns her attention to Mallory who by this time is on pins and needles. Shirley continues, although not reading now her voice lowers into the same even cadences as when she was reading.

"The tide comes and then it goes. You don't have to be born on a beach to know that!"

CHAPTER TWELVE

COURAGE

OF COWS AND MEN

"For the next ten years Mrs. Herschel visited the spot where her daughter was last seen. She tried to stop 'the back and forth' but something just dragged her there. Thaddeus, on those days she would first go to Portland where she attended the women's temperance meeting at the First Universal meetings rooms on Congress Square, Portland. That was the other part of her life trying to stop men from doing what they seem to be born to do: drinking, fighting and neglecting their children, real Maine men.

"Still adorned in white sash of the W.C.T.U., can you imagine, she would then take the train to Bath and end up in Phippsburg at Mrs. Anderson's boarding house and sit in her room overlooking the spot where Malaga waited in the water, Thaddeus. Sometimes, she would sit on the veranda like you do when you visit here. Anyhow, it was on the veranda where I met her. Our conversation began quite innocently. It was about the cicada. They seemed to be more in tune and less buzz like that year. We wondered if their song varies as to habitat, season and year. I told her that when my school children on the island capture them, they place them in a jar with fire flies. There is a dazzling effect at night.

"That's how we study the properties of sound and light in nature. She was shocked.

"Not only was she surprised that the half-cast offspring on the island could be taught anything, but she was mortified that a sensible woman like myself would have anything to encourage the notion that they could be taught.

"She insisted, as an eye witness, that they couldn't master even the simplest thing like swimming, a basic accomplishment of the most primitive tribes of Africa.

"It was when she told me about her daughter and the accident, I understood her anger. I remained silent. Capturing fire flies in a bottle cannot compete with tears. Just as quickly as her tears flowed down her cheek, they disappeared into the wrinkles of a curious smile.

"That's when she announced that it wouldn't be long before as she said 'impure things would be purified.' She said that there was a movement that was sweeping the nation. Even her union had vowed to forward the battle into Maine like they did with the temperance cause. The W.C.T.U. session earlier that day was inspired by a reprinted article written by a Bowdoin professor trumpeting the necessity of purity in civilization. She took a folded newspaper column from her purse and handed it to me. Just then Thaddeus, you came up the stairs, head buried in a book. You bumped into Mr. Arthur, the botanist who excused himself by addressing you by name in the most unflattering tone. It was the same name of the man who had written the article. Here it is!" Shirley waves the old newspaper strip in the air. "I thought I had lost it then during one of those trips for tea but it popped up." A little guilt and empathy slide across Shirley's eyes. "Remember this, sir?"

Instantly, Mallory realizes that he has been found out and attempts to withdraw to the farthest corner of the divan. The woman beside him had known who he was all along. He really didn't want to hear what he had written

Courage

but he was too slow to stop her. So Shirley reads:

PORTLAND GLOBE

PLINY'S AND HIS COWS

READERS

There is much gossip about the decay of the American Civilization. In doing so, comparison is made to the rise and fall of the Roman Empire, even though this nation of ours is barely over a century and a half it as compared to the thousand year reign of the latter. Many say, especially the ones who attend temperance meetings that the licentiousness and debauchery of our modern era surpass the days of Caligula. Now that's going some. For those readers who know their history, Rome fell not only because invading hordes of barbarians breached its borders and defeated its armies. It fell slowly and painfully to compromise and concession as it lost touch with its true virtues. The Roman way became weakened by foreign cultures and feebleminded inheritances. Even Pliny, the great Roman Historian and Statesman, was so disgusted with the drunkenness, blood sports and hypocrisies of the city, he fled to his province in the countryside to seek peace. It was a province just like our State of Maine.

His favorite pastime was to gaze upon the herd of white noble bred cows roaming the hillside, just like many of you readers in Washington, Aroostook and Penobscot counties do when you're resting.

He knew the secret to the preservation of Roman

The Malaga Chronicles

Civilization was in its husbandry of purity. In those ancient days the half breeds, the persons of low intelligence, the immigrants from poor parasitic countries were a menace even as they are now.

Today they are as much a threat to the purity of white Christian America as the evils of alcoholic spirits. I ask you women of the temperance movement once you achieve your goal and wipe out the entire inventory of spirits from this over burdened planet will our mothers, wives and children of our beloved State of Maine be really safe from the ignorant and socially undesirable from which their liquor breeds. Certain towns in our State have an unusually high number of vagrants, feebleminded and persons of color. Crime is rampant and municipal treasuries over burden. Groups should be organized to address this problem modeled after the many organizations that encourage that indolent population. Temperance committees should also join the Crusade. Deportation, expulsion and confinement, although drastic should not be overlooked. It is not just Darwin's survival of the fittest; it is survival of the purest. Pliny had the answer when he saw the cows but it was too late for Rome. What about Maine?

Thaddeus L. Mallory, Ph.D.
Guest Columnist Brunswick

"That was written thirty years ago, Shirley believe me! Someone found it and made it current to prove a point maybe that the wicked liberals of Bowdoin were social Darwinians or something."

"When I read it in the paper last month I couldn't

96

believe it. I certainly don't subscribe to that ballyhoo now, God forbid! At the time my mother was so upset that women didn't get the vote she blamed it on the Irish and the Downeast French. Since that time I found out that Pliny was a fraud. You know those white cows?

"They had white hair all right but black skin underneath. But they were so pure bred over the centuries that now they don't even give milk, in modern times they are mostly butchered for their meat!" Mallory faces Shirley for the first time since the article was read. "I feel guilty about that article enough so that I feel that I had some part in what happened here."

"You shouldn't my poor man. True, the temperance leagues are part of the ground swell that led to the expulsion of the poor souls from Malaga. Yet that poor woman that afternoon had in her purse another article more directly responsible for what happened." Shirley rises from the divan and like a sad town crier with more than a little sarcasm reads the clipping.

BATH INDEPENDENT

NOT FIT FOR DOGS. LIFE ON MALAGA

Poverty, immorality and disease. Disgusting and pitiable. A population of 35, and 26 of them sick with measles. No food, no beds, no fuel and scant shelter all winter long. Ignorance, shiftlessness, filth and heathenism.

A shameless disgrace that should be looked into at

once. The town of Phippsburg disowns these creatures and they are made outcasts.

"See when Governor Plaisted announced his plans of expulsion among other things he had that article in mind, and of course, he had in mind me, Shirley Alice Shapleigh!" Shirley's face shifts. Sadness crawls across her forehead to find uncharted space.

"Thaddeus, I have a confession to make?" They are closer on the divan now and she touches his hand. "You revealed yourself to me even though I knew little of the truth. I knew who you were back at Scanlon's. I more than guessed, after I looked into your lovely eyes, I knew that you came here not for amusement like the rest of them but for atonement."

"Is that your confession?"

"Hardly, well earlier," as she cleared her throat, "remember I told you about how I was inspired by Mrs. Lowell to teach the poor unfortunate children of Malaga, well it didn't happen just like that. When I returned home I learned how the town selectmen were looking for a teacher for the children on Malaga. I thought it was fate. Excitedly, I informed them that I was interested in the position but when I was taken to the island for the first time I was horrified.

"The island seemed to be just rocks slung together with moss and stunted trees that accidentally stuck out in the basin of the tide hole. As we reached the settlement of huts all I saw were pine slats folded over each other rising from mud foundations. The people I met there were dull and listless.

Courage

"I remind you that these were all first impressions you know. When I was introduced to the children who were indistinguishable from the rags they wore, I was very disappointed.

"They tried to recite the Pledge of Allegiance but I was met with a chorus of thick tongue stutters. Not one knew their alphabets or that Malaga was not a country. They hadn't even heard of Good Old Abe Lincoln mistaking him for a kind of cow.

"When I returned to the Town Hall I withdrew my application and informed the interviewing committee that the situation on the island was dire and that a school was the least of the Island's needs. What I really regretted was that I told them, in my opinion, the children were incapable of learning even the most simplest of tasks. Later in that same week I was proudly informed that a transcript of my interview with the selectmen was included in the petition of the town to divest itself of the island. That's how the State of Maine got involved in this mess."

Tears welled up in Shirley's eyes and fell down her cheeks. She hurried into the kitchen and when she returned with a steaming kettle the tears had fallen. She replenished the tea pot. Mallory's response first was silence then he realized what he had just heard:

"I don't understand, Shirley, I thought you were the teacher?"

"That came later, when I came to my senses, or after I received that letter from Cousin Sarah. Now Sarah, you'd love her. Although, she is the age of my aunt her spirit is as young as an older sister if I had one. The family calls her odd, very odd. She runs what you could call an asylum for intellectuals, philosophers and religious

99

nuts in Eliot near the New Hampshire border.

"If you go there you might see a Sultan standing on his head chanting on the front lawn, or you might hear hidden words falling from tongues in a way you never heard before."

"What in the world did she write that had that much of an impact on you?"

"It wasn't what she wrote it was what she didn't. First of all she was aware of the crazy things that were happening up here. The Portland newspapers were full of it. In Maine it is rare to have a township voluntarily throw away some of its off shore property regardless of how gnarled the politics may be.

"She also knew about the plight of the poor on Malaga. There were derogatory post cards circulating everywhere depicting their primitive condition in Maine, quite embarrassing for a state that had lost so many in a war to put an end to the same conditions that it trumpeted as a tourist attraction.

"Sarah indicated that she wished she could help them but could pray for them three times a day. She described the new religion she had embraced as very oriental. The teaching claims that 'God created all and all are His children.' It stands to reason that if God provides for us without discrimination how can we discriminate? She quoted something so profound that I memorized it verbatim. *Some are imperfect; they must be perfected. The ignorant must be taught, the sick healed, the sleepers awakened. The child must not be oppressed or censured because it is undeveloped; it must be patiently trained.*

"Then she wrote about many other things mostly spiritual but she never told me to do anything about Malaga. I suppose she knew what they say in and about here, 'Can't push somethun wit a rope,' had some truth in it. That's when I knew I had to go back there.

"The skiff pulled up on the shore of an island I didn't recognize. The trees once barren bloomed green, their dry leaves turned into flowers, and the homes sparkling, flooded with the sun. As I approached the inhabitants they greeted me with smiles of hope and the children not only did they know their alphabets, they sung them and when I asked if they still thought Malaga was a country, they all laughed and shouted even the littlest of them—that their Malaga was an island in Paradise. But they were quick to add, mind you, Maine."

Finally Mallory looks up, his remorse tempered. He smiles broadly. He laughs then she laughs. "What frauds we are Professor Mallory."

"What fraud this civilization is!" An astonished Mallory blurts out. "I never thought I'd say that!"

"Don't be embarrassed, Thaddeus. These are the times when we all should take heed to the shenanigans against nature that are happening all around us. Look at the *Titanic* and those poor souls. The proof is no one can conquer the sea; see what just happened and they are trying to make a better man nowadays by throwing away broken ones." It is as if Shirley is released from the opaque image of what she thought of herself. She stands and addresses Mallory.

"Do you know there was a group of New Englanders in the early 1800's who thought that by sweeping away the forests and leveling the hillsides there would a benefit? Our continent would be one great fertile womb. Warm winds would blow up from the South and cool winds would breeze down from the North. A man could get on his horse and just ride toward the sunset. Cattle would need no fences to hem them in. The rain could come when you wanted it to.

"The Indian problem would be solved because they would have nowhere to hide, an added benefit. It would be a world of perpetual summer. We figured out everything. Do you know what God did just to spite them? He saw to it that a pile of snow was dumped right on top of them in June."

"It snowed in June?"

"Right here in New England. That was the day Daniel Webster got religion they say. That was a hundred years ago and point taken. Now I think we better get going and take you back to that ivory tower of yours."

"But I'm not ready yet. I want you to read that last story, the one that must have been placed in the book that the boy slipped you this afternoon."

"I haven't even read it yet."

"All the more reason why it probably will be the last tale that will ever come from that island, you shouldn't read it alone."

Shirley thinks about it then goes to the side table where she placed it before she retrieved the newspaper clipping. She returns to the divan and opens the book.

CHAPTER THIRTEEN

HOPE

SPECIAL BOY

His fingers pushed aside the rock weed and Irish moss that clutched the bottom limbs of the magic reed he was about to harvest. Although a boy of seven, he had been carefully taught to survey the marsh north of the meadow for candidates. When he found one, he would approach it like he would a stranger talking to it, praising it and reasoning with it before it was pulled and wrapped in the newspaper sheet. He was a special boy and that's what they called him, owing to what purpose for which he had been selected. He could not have exclusive allegiance to any of the families on the island. He could play with the other children; he could go to school and he could go anywhere he wanted on the island, but he had to sleep in a different home every night, the same with his meals. That's how things were with Special Boy who brought the reeds to the council so that they could make decisions and make things work. He always stood in the corner of the king's parlor. And after a lot of the discussions back and forth he was summoned out of the shadows.

Solid metal bolts at the corners held together a harvest table. Over it a faded print of Queen Victoria presided, next to it ran a tile back splash behind a wash basin totally out of place. Facing Special Boy in mismatched upholstered chairs sat an assortment of puffed-cheeked, pumpkin faced men and one woman representing the island's families. Again they beckoned him in.

"Wants the sticks, sirs?" Special Boy presented the newspaper like quiver. The sun even though muted by the overcast shimmered through the seeded glass as it magnified Mr. Tolman, Mr. Lacey, Mother Washington, Mr. Bower, and King Conner.

"I still don't know what we are voting for. You can't have an ocean 'cept at sea level." Tolman had always been the one on the council who disagreed just to disagree and even though, at that crucial time, he still hadn't changed. On the table was the letter from Governor Plaisted. It was written as if no one at the table were capable of understanding it. It was written to be heard from someone more literate, like a sheriff.

"Paid more attention maybe everything would be as plain as the noses on our faces, you know." King Conner's deep barrel voice bounced off the table and woke up Joe Bower in the process.

Harold, who was sitting to the right of Tolman, just looked at the king and observed: "Many minds are like many winds, depends on the direction their blowing."

The king stood on his one leg and grabbed his crutch. He was a soldier who had fought in many battles and was all too ready to engage in another one. "July 1st they want us away from here. Should we stand and hold our ground or are we cowards and run, where should we run?"

Joe Bower slowly raised his sun browned hand, and then his head slightly lowered back to a resting position. Still, before he did he was able to mumble: "Count me in, gawd dag it!"

Mother Washington (sometimes she liked to be called Abigail) stood in all her glory. She was the head of the household for thirteen children, but over the years what she begot would have put the Bible to shame.

"We should have known better than to try to come to some decision today with Joe just off codin' on the Banks and Mr. Tolman here just coming off of some kind of delayed monthly visit from his monthly," she mused.

"I object to that, Abigail, and that which you are implying," Tolman squeaked.

"She ain't saying nothing new, Mr. Tolman. Seems over the decades you have made it your primary goal in life to disagree with anything there is to agree to and when we eventually agree with you, you disagree with that," the king explained. Tolman had a look of astonishment on his face but the king continued. "Now what do you mean by saying that you can't have an ocean except at sea level?"

"What he is saying in his queer way is "what is what is," there is nothing to vote about, we just got to leave," glared Mother Washington.

"You can't leave if you've left already!" added Harold who looked like a man who compromised on everything, even the shirt he wore. It was stained with pigswill, but if it had a collar he'd wear it to church.

"We got a lot to say about that like where are we going and how? That's all I am asking for is all of us here on the council to decide. But I warn you if we decide not to leave and hold our ground like men should do and women too, mother, there is going to be bloodshed!"

"I don't have much blood left!" Harold said under his breath.

"No, this time we have too many children!" Mr. Tolman warned.

"Where will we send them, there is only one way out and all of us have to go then, that's the price you pay for being different," observed Abigail with wisdom.

"They want us to fight them so they can come over here and wipe us out. They have always tried to get rid of us. They have sent teachers over here to try to cut off the roots of our past. That didn't work; we ended teaching the teachers." There rose a chorus of uh huh's. "They tried to send slave catchers in here, claiming that as runaways we were a fortune to be made. You know how that went. Most of those so-call fine southern gentlemen got so drunk they forgot what they were in Maine for." More uh huh's, and Abigail had barely got started. "Then they circulated this rumor about a treasure existing beneath the big cedar tree. That got a bunch of them over here from as far as away as Boston. They even brought boats the biggest ones could they fit in here without scraping bottom to put us all in. The only things they got were one gold tooth that the dogs dug up from Old William's grave and a whole batch of no see 'ums that got one so black that he had to show his birth certificate before they let him check into a Portland hotel." That fact was met with a lot of huzza's and laughter. "They even tried to steal our babies from us in plain sight by enticing them with parasols and smiles. They tried to murder us with work. They took us out on the fishing boats and we became the bait. But what got to me most of all was when they put that giant wolf on the island thinking that in panic we'd either flee or be killed by it. The only poor soul it got was April. Yet instead of discouraging us, and leaving us in disarray causing us to abandon our homes, April's death brought us more tightly together than ever."

"After that, lady and gentlemen I got to say we got a pullin' to do!" the king announced.

Hope

"What about Joe Bower here, King Conner?" Mr. Tolman questioned.

The king turned his big frame around and shouted into the adjoining room.

"Lottie, bring some of that Cat Cure in a basket for Mr. Bower!"

The cure must have been all made up, rolled up or stirred up or whatever one does to it to make it effective beforehand, because a woman almost a skinny as a string you could tie your pants up with came scurrying in, positioned a basket on the table and put one of Joe's hands in it. Everyone held their noses for a couple of seconds until Joe jumped up yelling, "Skunk!" Lottie laughed, blew around some powder, that she had clutched tightly in her other palm, and left with the basket beaming.

"Works every time, especially when you're laid up stiff like a poker. Suppose if I was dreaming I was on the Elysian Fields and about to..... and suddenly I thought I was patting a skunk; it would wake me up too." The king just said that because everybody knew Lottie used the Cat Cure in the basket on him plenty of times. He also was giving Joe sometime to realign himself to journey into the deeper dream of being there. "Now I see Joe here is back with us. Let's do it!"

"Do what?" Joe blurted out.

"Make the decision as to whether we are going to move ourselves out of here or stay another summer and stand our ground until frost bites?"

King motioned to Special Boy, who was standing in the corner witnessing the entire exchange in bewilderment, to come forward.

"Now who is going to be matched up with whom?"

king asked.

"I'd be with anyone except that fool." Abigail pointed to Tolman. "Although I love him, after all he is my cousin but only half the time. In the day time the truth is out."

"All right, you and Harold then!" The king took the quiver of reeds and offered it to Abigail who hesitated. "Do it, woman!"

"I was just thinking of a powerful conjure and just as I was, one came to mind." The large woman moved to the center of the room shaking. Her head went left to right, her huge butt went right to left, and her toes hit the old plank floor like they were drumming in a Penobscot corn dance. She slowly closed her eyes. When they were squinting tight her fingers flashed out and like lighting pulled out a bundle of reeds. She blew on them as if they had just caught the spark of an invisible fire.

"Are you sure?" the king bellowed.

"Just as sure as June comes hunting May!" The woman walked away clutching her choices beaming like they were prizes.

"Count 'em boy!" the king commanded. Special Boy's left arm surrounded the quiver as his right hand carefully counted the remaining reeds. "How many left boy?"

"Thirty-one, King Conner. There are thirty-one!" the boy announced.

"Recount!" Mr. Tolman blurted out as if on cue.

"There is no recount on this. We agreed to that a long time ago. That's why we got the boy. The boy gathers fifty-one reeds of the same length and the player who can pull out an even number of them without looking is the winner and gets one of the final says. If there is a tie, the one with the highest number of reeds in his hand is the victor. Remember that's why we trust the boy and his count." The king reminded them.

"Besides Mr. Tolman, what kind of say do you have on anything that has to do with this round? Harold is my match." Abigail had to throw her two cents in as she was returning her reeds to the quiver.

"Harold it's your turn! Harold...HAROLD!" The king glared at Harold. "I thought that Joe here was the only one who had been sleeping in a hill of beans?"

"I don't want to!" Harold whined, his hands hidden beneath each arm pit. "Whenever I win and think I have the last say, you get to say the last say after me!"

"That's only because your last say isn't saying anything."

Of course, everybody else in that small parlor laughed because they knew it was the true state of their government.

"Tell me now; tell me when I overruled your last say?"

"Remember when Grey Gull, White Wing's boy, used to fly over the shit house all the time dropping bird do and I had the last *say*? Well, I said shoot it down."

"I disagreed with that one." Mr. Tolman piped in.

"We did what you directed we shot it down." King Conner retorted with a good idea as to what Harold was getting at.

"Months later we shot it down!" Harold continued. "It was only after it dropped bird do on you while you were in the shit house shittin' did we shoot it down!"

"The wheels of justice work real slow. Anyhow it turned out that it was the wrong decision in the first place because White Wing seems to have taken up a mad revenge and is flying around the island right now, *bird doing* on anything that doesn't have a cover."

"Last week it got me right on the head!" Lottie hollered from the adjoining room.

"Anyhow you got to go through with it Harold. That's democracy! Maybe we got to have a last say pulling on that?" Mr. Tolman said who was sometimes good at stirring up trouble.

"Wait a minute we're not going to have a last say pulling, on whether or not to have a last say on something entirely different?" Abigail was heated. "The way I see it I won. I'm not doing any more pulling today!"

"I guess that settles it, and unless anyone disagrees other than Mr. Tolman, we are going to finally have the last say about leaving this island." The king took a deep breath waved his arms and shouted: "Lottie, bring out the book."

Lottie must have been waiting all that time in the adjoining room cradling the pillow upon which the book rested. The pillow was encrusted with a golden flower pattern interweaved into its velvet cloth. A braid of gold and silver ran across its dimensions giving way to the tassels that dangled from the four corners of its bottom designed to render invisible any hand that carried it so it would appear that it was floating.

"Guess this is it" were the only words Lottie said as she placed the pillow with the book in the middle of the table. Then she scurried off not wanting to know, see or hear anything about what was about to take place.

Joe, Abigail Washington, Harold and Mr. Tolman all stood around the table. King Conner went up to the boy who was patiently waiting and said: "You did well now come back in a half an hour. Your services will be needed again." The king returned to the table and reached for the palms of his friends. He completed the circle of the ancient ritual.

As Special Boy sat on the rock that the king had rolled to the back side of his cabin, he heard moaning and groaning and other unearthly sounds. Like they say, "Who can distinguish between devils praying and angels begging?"

He sat on that rock and kicked the pebbles at his feet as he heard the usual sounds he always heard after a pullin', the only difference was the voice heard above it all. Sometimes it was Harold's, sometimes it was the king's, sometimes it was a voice he had never heard before, still it was a voice that could have belonged to anyone on the council or anyone or thing not of this world. This time it was Mother Washington's and just as the moaning began it stopped. She said: "I say we have that last say and that is to go and not let any of them flatlanders have the everlasting satisfaction of seeing us shuffling across their faces helpless and beaten!"

"Your lips are flapping now woman but put it in the book!" shouted the now wide awake voice of Joe Bower while other voices mumbled in agreement. There was a long silence above some activity before another voice added: "Now, mother, you must tell us why you come to that decision, so to speak, and put that down in the book too. You know that and here is me telling you." Right then the moaning and groaning started up again.

Suddenly Abigail's voice broke out loud and clear, just as purposeful as it was before but it was in this weird way like it was a continuation of a story that had been told before:

CHAPTER FOURTEEN

PURITAN HISTORY

"Now this happened way back, way back before there was a way back," as Abigail spoke music slipped into the room. *To be honest she kind of hummed this.*

"To Tela their bodies just didn't fit right, at least not like the body of Sema, the boy from the other band of Africans that moved across the sea with them had fit. A woman wants to disappear into the body of her man before he can do it and claim her possession without him knowing it.

"Her mate was from the 'Ancients' the stocky men, they call them now Neanderthals.

"They trapped bison on the plateau above and in sheer numbers confused lions while they stole their prey. They all lived in the world where Malaga Spain now stands and spreads along the lips of the Mediterranean Sea. His name was Auyan, white as one could tell beneath the black fur that cocooned his body. He held Tela like he always held things. Let us just say that she taught him about loving and its sacrifice and he taught her about holding on to something to the bitter end. They could have lasted for years trying to snuggle up like that but they had heard the dogs and how they barked angrily lunging forward searching for them and their little children.

"Tela's father had been furious with her coupling with Auyan. Auyan was so different from the rest of her family. His family was of another kind. Short armed and stunted leg, no good for running or spearing, fingers too stubby to fondle the earth, memory so weak that most had the same name if they could remember it. As I said they call them now Neanderthals.

"Her father had led raids on Ancient's settlements, witnessing the bodies of old males and females tossed over the cliffs along with whatever blunt headed children his sons could find. Afterward he would gather up their crude belongings to see if they had any secret he didn't know so that he could destroy any sign that they even existed. Eventually, Tela's father would see to it that all of them were burned and tossed into the sea.

"It was years before when Tela found Auyan between the cracks of boulders that stood guard above the sand field which tumbled down to meet the sea. She was about to call to her brothers who had trailed ahead to find Ancients.

"But then she saw Auyan's blue eyes. They shined through his low overhung brows like shafts of blue light and poured into hers like nothing else ever had. Not even the moon in the Andalusian night had touched her heart like they had.

"Her father promised her that once they crossed the sea she would find a mate, Sema was whom he had in mind. Sema was his brother's son. Once the land had been cleared of Ancients, Sema and Tela would raise a family of their own and live as long as he and his mate had lived, and their children would have children and their children would have children. When she saw Auyan's eyes she knew that would never be.

"During the time Auyan remained hidden Tela would bring him food, such as dates, nuts, berries and roots. But he needed meat. So she fed him the fresh remains of the small animals her family kept for skins. She explained to her brothers that she had found a lame dog which refused to leave its shelter and she was feeding it.

"As the months went by her stomach grew with child. That's how Auyan was discovered. As the year passed Tela's suspicious mother with her sons followed her expecting to see an unspeakable beast found something to them that was much worse. The figure cuddled in the warm skins was a child that looked just like them but with the bluest eyes that they had ever seen. Because Auyan bravely stepped forward to protect his child he forced Tela's brother to back away in astonishment and in a way admiration. Tela's mother instinctually wept and took the baby in her arms and held it. Where was the beast that they were told such a mating would produce? Were these creatures that they were hunting down and killing, were they human after all?

"Now, Tela's clan was a clan that would inherit its destiny. They came up to the sea chasing antelope from deep in Africa but kept a northern trail as the animals veered east when the winds pushed the rivers in that direction. The only way they survived was through cooperation and mutual respect. The clan had one rule that wove through the tapestry of its generations—'Never kill your own blood, regardless of the circumstances.' Therefore, Tela's father only cursed her and her lover and vented his wrath by throwing stones in the air to open up the eyes of the gods so they could see what they had done. And the next day when the sun with all its glory only came up unrepentant the clan left the plateau where they had found a home and moved northward leaving Tela and her child with Auyan to take care of them in a shelter overlooking the Mediterranean.

"For the most part they were forgotten and everyone went on with their living. But Sema did not forget, he swore that he would return one day with others of different blood and settle things.

"As years went by, Tela and Auyan were joined by other families like them. In the day they not only fished and hunted, because they combined their diets and ate roots and berries with their meat, they grew crops and kept animals.

"At night they gathered in huge caverns for protection. Within the hills of el Torcal they built a city with limestone and rain. On the walls of the city they wrote a book. It was the first book. In it, even the seal and the antelope, their gods of sustenance, looked toward a greater, unknown essence.

**

"Soon the strange rocks and grass plains of Nerja became alive with flowers and trees while underneath them children of a different kind dreamed. One night a messenger from Tela's father came to warn her that Sema had gathered up a horde of murders and plunderers and was approaching. Tela laughed and shouted why run when they see us and see what we have done and the paradise we have made, they will treat us as equals. The other families, heeding Tela's father's warnings, did not look to Tela and Auyan for direction. They dug into an immense cavern and they called it their world and in fear they dug so deep not stopping until they saw the stars. Sema came with vengeance, blocking all the caves forcing the remaining colonists into the sea.

"For Auyan and his former lover Tela, Sema had a special thing planned. He buried them alive up to their lips in the sand and as the tide rose, sand filled their stomachs. When the water reached Tela's eyes, salt from tears poured out and when it reached Auyan, his eyes poured out blue.

"As the centuries passed, on that beach the Phoenicians erected a great city. They called that city Malaga. They rested there before they passed through the Pillars of Hercules and entered a new world.

"For centuries anyone who was different from the people of the times: Greek, Roman, African, Muslim or Catholic and Protestant, upon death their bodies were buried upright in the sand."

Mother Washington finally sermonized at the end with a standing "Halleluiah!"

"Good, that's a lesson learned. Put all of it in the book!" An unidentified voice hollered. "Halleluiah!"

"Halleluiah!" shouted more.

"She can talk the paint off a barn wall," said another.

"Also put in the book that before all of it, the Mediterranean was this ugly muddy color and fresh, was wicked fresh as a baby's pee!" a voice that sounded like Harold's piped in as if he had been there and seen it firsthand.

CHAPTER FIFTEEN

THE BOOK

A large arm stuck out of the back door of King Conner's cabin and beckoned Special Boy. As he entered he saw Abigail was finishing whatever she was putting in the book while the others were either, stretching, squirming or kicking back in their chairs. One stood, another glared at him, and a third stared at the roof, deep in thought.

"What good was leaving Teacher the book? Did she ever show anyone, other than the children, the tales?" Harold turned and directed his question to the king.

"Hard to say, some of the rumors got out there. But one day she'll realize who she is." The king just shrugged and motioned for the quiver of reeds the boy was clutching.

"Now we have another final say to make now that we know that we are going, now the question is how are we going and where. Mr. Tolman you are matched to Joe with that one. Pull, you first Joe!"

Joe stepped up to the king but unlike Abigail he didn't dance or conjure. He just reached his hand out and pulled up a bunch of reeds.

"Count them reeds boy!" Joe commanded. The king handed the quiver to Special Boy and he counted them as fast as grease slicks a wagon wheel.

"Sir, he came up odd and he grabbed twenty-five!" the boy mumbled. Joe quickly counted his reeds and when he came to twenty-five he tossed all of them on the table and walked away.

"Come on, Mr. Tolman, you're next." As the boy

picked up the reeds and put them in the quiver, the king approached Tolman with a broad smile on his face. Tolman's first name was Francis. He had out lived his wife and two of his children and one grand baby who didn't even live long enough to see what the fuss was all about. People always called him Mister Tolman because it sounded right. He always wore a plaid vest even when he was on the lee side of a boat hauling traps as the wind slapped pass. He ran away from Skowhegan when he was very young and went to camp with hunters. Although he was half Indian he acted more like the other half, so Abenaki didn't want him either. That's why he questioned everything. He wanted to find the answer for himself. It was a matter of trust.

"Pull it, Francis!" The king was getting impatient.

"Look at him; he's moving like a female lobster full of tail!" Abigail snickered.

Tolman moved about a foot from the quiver the boy was now holding and without a bit of conjure much like Joe, plunged his hand into the reeds and took out his share.

"Just don't stand there boy, count 'em."

"He got an even pull with thirty-one remaining!" Everyone was hoping that Mr. Tolman would do well, even Abigail deep down. The only one who was hoping the opposite was Mr. Tolman.

"Tolman you looked like you were sent for and couldn't come!" The king said with a bit of suspicion rising. "It's your say. It's the final one. How are we going to get out of here?"

"You mean by boat toward Harpswell or take the shallow down by the Meadow?" Joe snickered. "Maybe we just wade, all of us wade into the town! What do you think? Maybe someone is gonna give us all fares to Brunswick?"

"Say you, Tolman. Say you?"

He just looked at the king and shrugged.

"If you figure out this one maybe you'll be able figure out what else is coming." Abigail shook her head and sat down in disgust.

"Can't believe it, he doesn't have anything to say or is it because he doesn't want to have the last say because he himself will disagree with it."

It finally sunk into Harold, the degree of difficulty they were in, that is. Mr. Tolman just kept his mouth clamped tight, eyes peeling the ceiling boards. It was the first time that it had happen in a long time and even then maybe it didn't happen. "Joe should do the pullin' again?"

"He doesn't have to that's why I am here?" The king stood and hopped toward him.

"You are not that kind of king. This whole 'last say,' pullin' is not about who's running the rudder. Why would we have a council? We've gone through centuries without one...Italy, Phoenicia, and Spain. Kings, queens and generals were all we needed. Then we come to America, here voting is how one decides by. Even that doesn't work, too much arguing. Everybody wants to vote, even the women." Harold was boiling mad now. "Now we all agreed to this reed pullin' idea, you know. The simplest way, the spiritual way, the Indian way and the only one who decides is Good Godfrey and maybe, just maybe, Special Boy!"

"Look whose yapping....you gave up your pull just a minute ago," says the king.

"Maybe I should be the one who should pull. I'm the

only woman! I am the only other one that got an even pull and accepted it." Abigail slid the book back to her and stood. Suddenly she glanced down: "Look at this", she shouted. "In the space after I scrawled into the book just a minute ago mind you, there is writing and it isn't mine!"

"The book got tired of you old fools deciding and is writing itself its own story!" Lottie shouted from the adjoining room. The jaws in that room dropped like a bunch of loggers let loose at a clam bake!

The king approached balancing on his crutch, he squinted one eye until the shape of the writing focused clearly.

I went into a piece of paradise. I walked in a most lovely garden. Here were myrtle hedges with blooms for thousands of bridal wreaths; tall geranium bushes encircled memorial tablets. Passion flowers twined their tendrils over many gravestone and pepper trees drooped their weeping branches over many a resting place. Here stood a solitary palm, there a rubber tree. Pretty children with laughing eyes played there. The whole garden is encircled by a hedge of wild cactus, over which one looks down to the broad, rolling sea.

Hans Christen Andersen wrote that about a cemetery of another Malaga in 1862, seems that all the Malagas are the same, Good Godfrey!

The air was silent, and the bickering just proved human after all. Special Boy who was still in the parlor had the final say: "Wasn't all you folk doing was just writing fairy tales, anyhow?

Well, that just proved that Special Boy was the wisest of them all.

120

CHAPTER SIXTEEN

HOLES

There are holes in the heart
Like in the earth
In which one waits the true gold?

Shirley stops reading.

"What?" Mallory tries to peer over her shoulder to see for himself.

"It says that the next part is not supposed to be read except by me."

"Why? I can see it myself. All it says is at the end is they dug a hole."

Startled, Shirley closes the book and stands.

"True, that's why they brought Goodboy back! What they mean is I probably would be the only one who would understand."

"Understand what?"

"The children's favorite book, I had to read it over and over again."

"What?"

"It was Hans Christen Andersen's, *The Steadfast Tin Soldier*. What else could they do? Where else can broken things go but deep into the breast of the earth so that they can be born again when they go through the fire that's at the heart of the earth."

"Below?"

"There are tunnels in the earth like in the imagination. They say that's how some of them got here. They didn't come through Ellis Island believe you me.

"You haven't seen all of them you know. You only

have seen those of them who have come into town. After all, you can call a rose grotesque if you are blind and pick it up with your fingers. "

One of her fingers begins to wave like the fingers of well-bred women sometimes do when there is something really important to tell and that there is no other way to get the attention of their well-bred men.

"They took away a whole family last month just because they looked different. But the children were the smartest in the class, way above their age level.

"What a cruel thing prejudice is especially when it is thought to be the right thing to do. It saddens me the most that it is being done by enlightened people like us, everyday. What makes me furious are those who in turning a blind eye think they are superior. Worse are those who are like us, who know and wait and prefer to live their lonely lives rather than to get involved. "

Mallory doesn't reply in his customary manner with words, wrapping her in his arms was good enough. He guides her to the divan.

"Who brings joy to my heart are those who repent and take action of some kind or another and realize that the most supernatural thing of all is love." She whispers in his ear as the whispers become brushes on lips and the brushes become touches. They hold each other tightly as if they are about to merge. Unexpectedly or expectedly in character Shirley breaks away taking a deep breath as she does.

"That was a modern thing to do. I've only known you for an afternoon."

"It is not shameful. It seems that I have known you for like Scheherazade, a thousand and one afternoons and your tales have entrapped me. I have to warn you

that I am a confirmed bachelor at least I thought I was."
He stands, stretches his legs and walks to the window.

"I would say that you should have learned that at least from what you heard today."

"You say ......?" sputters Mallory as he looks out the window.

"...miracles...about miracles?" she muses.

"Speaking of miracles. Shirley, come look. It's snowing!"

TO SUM UP

Death, to some
Is summing up life
To decide
Whether not
To go on,
They never think
Like it or not
They will.

Of course, it wasn't snowing in June of 1912. When George Pease was sent by the Governor to evict whoever was left on the island he had arrived early and found not one soul. He burned all of the remaining structures down except the schoolhouse. It was the ashes that looked like snow coming down. Mallory and Shirley found out the hard way when they ran outside to make a snowman. The good thing was that for both of them it was completely out of character. I suppose the miracle of love had something to do with it. Anyhow they had a wedding a couple of years later at her Cousin Sarah's place in Eliot, Maine called Green Acre. Green Acre, unlike the houses on Malaga and the *humans* associated with this story, is still there. That's where they talk about things like this. As for the special people from the island, a lot of them are still around, few know who they really are.

However others were sighted living and fishing in their soiled underwear on the Shoals south of Portland, while others were spotted down in New Jersey fishing for bass and kissing them before they let them go and still others were seen as far away as Washington State pulling in steelhead rainbow trout in order to have lunch with them beneath picnic trees.

It wasn't strange at all that all the places they dug up to were called Malaga, or its other name, *Salt* (as in tears), like those who settled in California, and dug up their lives from the faults around the Salton Sea.

As for Mallory and Shirley, they honeymooned in Malaga, Spain and spent time looking at the stalagmites growing in the great caverns in Pileta to see if she spotted anyone she knew. When they returned back to Maine they took teaching positions, up in the Unrecognized Territories, telling children of logging folks about the outside world by telling them first about the one inside.

I suppose once a Teacher always one.

NOTE TO THE READER

I couldn't end this short book just like that. I summed up everything except what happened to the island, real or imagined. After a hundred years, things and places we call real, become myth and visa versa. What about the island's destiny?

By the time the archeologists and the historians started digging into things, the Land Trust people had adopted it and opened it to everyone. A couple of years ago a crusty old fisherman took my wife and I to that 'spit of land stickin' up in the tide hole'. "All these people comin to see it, baffles me," he remarked: "Don't see much to it." Maybe some would agree with him but I, without even trying, could see Miss Shapleigh's children hiding up in the cedars.

"There are tunnels in the earth like in the imagination. They say that's how some of them got here. They didn't come through Ellis Island believe you me."

HISTORICAL NOTES

- As I noted in my foreword, this book is not about the historical Malaga, ME. The setting is a platform to inspire the discussion on Eugenics and Race in a poetic way. There were no parades. Actually the residents of the island had approximately a year to leave.
- There was a strong element of racial prejudice in the area. In nearby Bath, Maine, a KKK clan had a strong following. Temperance groups had affiliations with national KKK women's organizations on the executive level. Social welfare groups and white purity leagues worked together.
- In 1905 the U.S. government created the Heredity Commission to increase the families of good blood.
- The island school was a good school according to the standards of the day. The teacher was Lucy Lane who also worked with her father Charles Lane to provide social services to the tiny village.
- The residents called James McKinney the king. He allegedly cooperated with the state and was responsible for the admission of some residents to the Pineland Center for the Feeble Minded.
- Phippsburg was founded many years after King William's War. During the war the prior settlement was decimated by the Abenaki, established on the site of the first attempted English colony in New England.
- June snow fell in New England in 1816.
- Pre-Colombian Scandinavian rune stones were found in the area. Thingstones and runes sparked the imagination of Hans Christian Andersen. Incredible natural People Shape thingstones are found in Malaga Spain (menhir). The Abenaki called Malaga, Mologo for centuries. It means Standing People.

- Andersen loved Malaga, Spain. Malaga, Spain loved him; there is a statue of him in the center of the city.

- The English cemetery in Malaga, Spain was established because Catholic burial grounds were off-limits and Protestants were buried in the sand upright, symbolically exiling them into the sea.

- Sarah Farmer was one of the first adherents of the Baha'i Faith in Maine. Some of her ancestors were Shapleigh's and responsible for the first recorded slave transaction in Maine.

- The son of Baha'u'llah, Abdul'baha, visited Sarah at her retreat, John Whittier Greenleaf named, Green Acre in 1912 during his only visit to the West. His purpose was to teach the Oneness of Mankind.

- In 1912-15 Alfred Wegener completed his theory Origins of Continents and Oceans and the mega continent, Pangaea.

- There was an Indian Game described as pulling straws played in various ways across the continent.

REFERENCES

'Abdul-Baha.' "['*The Secret of Divine Civilization, Selections*']." Education Today (Taipei) (2 17 Aug. 1984)
'Abdul-Baha' and (Abdul Baha Abbas). "'America and World Peace'." The Independent Vol.73 (**September 5, 1912**): 'Abdul-Baha' and Compiled by Howard MacNutt. The Promulgation of Universal Peace. 1st. reprinted 1922 [i.e. 1939], 2 vols. in 1, New York.

Aubet, María Eugenia. *The Phoenicians and the West: politics, colonies and trade.* Cambridge University Press

Bredsdorff E. *"Andersen H.C.: Story of His Life"* Noonday Press. 1992

Barkan, Elazar. The Retreat of Scientific Racism: Changing Concepts of Race in Britain and the United States between the World Wars. Cambridge, U.K.: Cambridge University Press, 1992.

Broberg, Gunnar, and Nils Roll-Hansen, eds. Eugenics and the Welfare State: Sterilization Policy in Denmark, Sweden, Norway, and Finland. East Lansing: Michigan State University Press, 1996.

Read more: Eugenics - Bibliography - Press, York, University, and Racism—JRank Articles:
http://science.jrank.org/pages/9252/Eugenics-BIBLIOGRA-PHY.html#ixzz1l4HXyfir
Lee, Maureen Elgersman, *Black Bangor: African Americans in a Maine Community, 1880-1950,* 2005, University Press of New

England, Hanover, N.H.

"Miss Farmer and Greenacre." The Open Court (Chicago) 29 **(Sept. 1915)**: 572.11.698

Gallagher, Nancy L., *Breeding Better Vermonters: The Eugenics Project in the Green Mountain State,* 1999, University Press of New England, Hanover, N.H.

Lights of Guidance: A Baha'i Reference File. comp. Helen Hornby. New Delhi: Baha'i Publishing Trust, 1983.

Kennedy, Randall, *Interracial Intimacies: Sex, Marriage, Identity, and Adoption,* 2003, Pantheon Books, New York.

Kimball, Richard S., *Pineland's Past: The First One Hundred Years,* 2001, Peter Randall, Portsmouth, N.H.

McBride, James, *The Color of Water: A Black Man's Tribute to His White Mother,* 1996, Riverhead Books, New York.

Mitchell, Steve, *The Shame of Maine: The Forced Eviction of Malaga Island Residents,* 1999, self-published, Brunswick, Maine.

Mitchell, Steve, *The Shame of Maine: Malaga—The Story Behind the Pictures,* 1999, self-published, Brunswick, Maine.
Mitchell, Steve, The Shame of Maine: What Ever Became of the Residents of Malaga?, 2005, self-published, Brunswick, Maine.

Mosher, John, *No Greater Abomination: Ethnicity, Class, and Power Relations on Malaga Island, Maine, 1880-1912,* 1991,

Masters Thesis, University of Southern Maine, American and New England Studies Program.

Phippsburg Historical Society, *Stories of Phippsburg, Maine, Vol. 2,* 2003.

Price and Talbot, *Maine's Visible Black History,* 2006, Tilbury House, Gardiner, Maine.

Riis, Jacob, *How The Other Half Lives,* 1997, Penguin Books, New York.

Schwarzbach, M. 1986. Alfred Wegener the father of continental drift. Science Tech, Madison, Wisconsin,

Sargent, Ruth, *Images of America: The Casco Bay Islands,* 1995, Arcadia Press, Dover, New Hampshire.

Schmidt, Gary, *Lizzie Bright and the Buckminster Boy,* 2006, Random House, New York.

Metzler, Chris and Springer, Jeff —"*Plagues & Pleasures on the Salton Sea"* Tilapia Film, [2006]—Thorough history of the first 100 years at the Salton Sea and the prospects for the future.

Sanchidrián, Jose Luis, of the University of Cordoba, Spain in *The New Scientist* February 2012 discusses Neanderthal Art in Caves in Malaga.